THE

AMULET

OF

AMON–RA

Leslie Carmichael

Children's Brains are Yummy Books
Austin, Texas

Children's Brains are Yummy Books
www.cbaybooks.com

The Amulet of Amon-Ra

Copyright © 2009 Leslie Carmichael
ISBN (10): 1-933767-11-1
ISBN (13): 978-1-933767-11-6

Library of Congress CIP data available.

Printed in the United States by United Graphics.
Job # 192183
Printed on Husky 60#

For my parents:

Alice May "Maisie" Williams (Weightman)
February 17, 1923 - August 12, 1992

Samuel Henry "Harry" Williams
May 28, 1918 - May 10, 1990

The mummy lay on its back, partially wrapped in faded linen bands. Its dark skin had dried tight against the bones of its bald skull, which had a few wisps of gray hair still attached. The mummy's only jewelry was a thin gold bracelet.

"Cool," said Jennifer Seeley. "Grandma, come look at this!"

"No, you have to come take a look at this!" said Grandma Jo.

Jennifer glanced at her grandmother, then back at the mummy. Despite its sunken cheeks and skeletal nose, it seemed familiar somehow, although she couldn't think why. Maybe she'd seen it in one of her books.

"Coming," she said, trotting across the carpet to her grandmother's side.

"Look," said Grandma Jo, pointing at a stone fragment fastened to the wall. "It says this is part of a tomb painting."

"So?"

"So, look closely."

Jennifer leaned forward. The painting was protected by a thin sheet of plastic. Its colors were still bright, though peeling. A young girl in a white dress stood in the typical ancient Egyptian pose, with shoulders and upper body flat, but head and legs turned to the right, as if she was walking.

The young girl's face was finely drawn. Jennifer's eyes widened as she realized why Grandma Jo had wanted her to see it.

"That girl looks like you, doesn't she?" Grandma Jo said, smiling. "Except that her hair is black, not brown. Isn't that interesting?"

"Yes," Jennifer whispered, reaching for the figure. She gasped as a spark of static electricity leapt from the plastic to her finger.

"They do say that everyone has a double somewhere," Grandma Jo continued cheerfully. "It looks like yours is thousands of years old."

Was that all it was? A double? Jennifer stared at the painting. Somehow, she wasn't sure.

"But how could I be in ancient Egypt?" she muttered, rubbing her finger.

2

"Excuse me."

"Eep!" said Jennifer.

She and her grandmother spun around, to see a gray-haired, dark-skinned man dressed in a three-piece suit.

"Oh!" said Grandma Jo. "You startled us!"

"I do beg your pardon," said the man. "I only meant to find out if you needed any help. May I tell you anything about the collection?"

"This painting," Jennifer began.

"Ah, yes. A fascinating example of tomb art. Quite unusual, actually—note the detailed features of the girl and woman. Most Egyptian art follows the traditional canon, but this has subtle differences. The artist must have been a master of his craft. The hieroglyphs are quite interesting as well. They tell the story of—"

"Daoud?" Grandma Jo interrupted. She was staring at the man. "Daoud, is that you?"

He squinted at Grandma Jo, then pulled a pair of glasses from his jacket pocket and slipped them on. His face brightened. "Miss Josephine!"

"Daoud, how wonderful to see you again, after all

3

these years!" Grandma Jo laughed. "You haven't changed a bit."

Daoud touched his gray hair. "My family is known for aging well," he said, grinning. His white teeth gleamed against his dark skin. "You are still lovely."

Grandma Jo giggled. Jennifer looked at her in astonishment. Grandma Jo, giggling?

"Who is this?" he asked, looking at Jennifer.

Grandma Jo gently prodded Jennifer forward. "My granddaughter, Jennifer. This is Daoud Elgabri. He was our tour guide, when I went on that trip to Egypt, long before you were born."

"Jennifer?" Daoud tilted his head to one side. "Ah, yes, I can see a resemblance."

"What are you doing in the United States?" asked Grandma Jo.

Daoud spread the fingers of his right hand over his chest and bowed slightly. "I am no longer a humble tour guide. You see before you a fully-trained Egyptologist."

"How wonderful!" Grandma Jo exclaimed. "I told you education would help you get ahead. Are you with this exhibit, then?"

4

"I have the honor of being in charge. And it is all thanks to you."

"Me?" Grandma Jo's eyebrows flew up.

"You and your friends' generous tips allowed me to begin my schooling," said Daoud.

"I'm so glad! You deserved them. You were such a good guide." She turned to Jennifer. "We saw things with him that we never would have even known existed."

Daoud smiled. "Allow me to show you once again. I can give you a personal tour of this collection."

"Just like you did in Egypt," said Grandma Jo. "But without dragging me into every bazaar you can find, this time."

"I seem to recall it was the other way around," said Daoud, winking at Jennifer. "I would be happy to tell you about this small part of my country's great heritage."

"That would be lovely. Wouldn't it, Jennifer?"

"Uh, sure," said Jennifer.

"I bet you'll find out more now than you would on your field trip. Her eighth grade class is coming here in a couple of weeks," Grandma Jo confided to Daoud.

"We have several school visits on the schedule," said

Daoud. "You couldn't wait?"

"We thought it would be quieter, especially on a Saturday morning," said Grandma Jo.

This way, Jennifer could actually look at the artifacts, without Hannah and Ashley trying to hustle her through as quickly as possible, and without Tyler trying to trip her at every opportunity.

Daoud's eyes crinkled. "I understand. Have you been studying my country in your class?"

"We just started," said Jennifer. "Mrs. Goodwin let us choose our own topics."

"And yours is?"

"The Pharaohs," said Jennifer. "Some of them, anyway."

"All great men," said Daoud. "All but one," he added, with a smile.

"You mean Hatshepsut," said Jennifer.

"Is there anything in this collection about them?" asked Grandma Jo.

"There is a little," said Daoud, "but most of these artifacts are from Nubia, rescued from the rising waters of Lake Nasser, which flooded much of the area when the Aswan Dam was completed. These artifacts do not travel much—not because they are rare or especially valuable, but because most people would rather see the more famous pieces."

"Like Tutankhamen's gold mask," said Jennifer.

"Precisely," said Daoud. "But I prefer the simpler things. They are so much better at telling us how the ordinary people lived, day to day."

He tucked Grandma Jo's arm in his and led her to a nearby display case. Jennifer, with a glance at the girl in the tomb painting, followed.

"These, for example," said Daoud, pointing to a collection of pots, spoons, and small dishes. "They were found in the tomb with the mummy. Can you guess what they are?"

Jennifer peered at the delicate jars and plates, all made of a buttery-yellow substance. A bronze disk, propped up behind them, made a blurry reflection of three slim stone rods. A set of dishes? No, too small.

"Are they for make-up?" Jennifer asked.

"Well done!" said Daoud. "Yes, they are cosmetics containers. The stoppered vessels were probably for perfumes. Long gone by now, of course. They were for use in the afterlife."

"I read they put food in the tombs for the mummies to eat and drink, too," said Jennifer.

"Yes, indeed. We even have some of that here," said Daoud. He pointed to another case that held small jugs with handles and pointed bottoms, and some round gray loaves. "They believed they needed the physical item or a representation to be comfortable. Of course, by now the bread is rock, the seeds petrified and wine only a stain in the amphorae."

"I would have thought it would be all crumbled to dust by now," said Grandma Jo.

"Dust, yes," said Daoud. "There is always dust. Like the mummies, they have dried out in the desert heat."

"Oh, it makes me thirsty just to think of it," said Grandma Jo. "I remember it was so hot, but it was so dry that the sweat just evaporated off of us."

Daoud chuckled. "I wish I could offer you a glass of ice-cold karkadeh."

"Mmm," said Grandma Jo. She answered Jennifer's unspoken question. "Hibiscus tea, cooled and sweetened. It's delicious."

"Perhaps you will visit Egypt someday, and taste it for yourself," said Daoud. "Meanwhile, let me show you the rest of this collection."

He drew them into a second room, which held more display cases, filled with the small figurines called ushabti, which were supposed to take the place of the dead in the fields of the gods, so they could take their ease in the afterlife. There were also dozens of amulets in the shapes of scarab beetles, animals, eyes of Horus, and the looped crosses called ankhs.

"Hundreds of amulets have been found all over Egypt, most of them originally entombed with the mummies," Daoud explained. "They were worn throughout life, and many more were wrapped in the layers of linen shrouds at the wearer's death, placed at throat, wrists and forehead. They were worn for protection and luck."

Standing as if they were guarding the room were several mannequins dressed as the gods and goddesses of ancient Egypt.

"I know these!" said Jennifer, recognizing them. "There's Isis, with the wings and half-moon headdress. That green-skinned guy is Osiris, her husband. He's wrapped in linen like a mummy, because he's Lord of the Dead. And there's Horus, their son, with the head of a hawk."

"He is flanked by two goddesses," Daoud said, smiling. "Hathor, the cow goddess; and lion-headed Sekhmet. Both were guardians of the young god."

By itself in a corner of the room was another mannequin, next to a stone scarab the size of a dinner plate. Like Horus, he was bare-chested but for a pectoral of colored beads, and he also wore a white pleated skirt, the Egyptian kilt. His head was topped by a tall, split crown.

"Who's that?" asked Jennifer.

"Amon-Ra, city-god of Thebes," said Daoud. "A handsome fellow, is he not?"

"At least he has a human head," said Grandma Jo.

"Mm, yes," said Daoud. "Now, let me show you the pride of our collection."

"The mummy?" asked Jennifer.

"Oh, must we?" asked Grandma Jo. "I'm not too fond of them."

"I thought you saw some when you went to Egypt," said Jennifer.

"Yes, but only animals. Some crocodiles and a cat. They were bad enough. Harriet was the one who went into the mummy room at the museum in Cairo." Grandma Jo shuddered. "They give me the willies."

"Well, I'd like to know about it," said Jennifer. "Was it found in the same tomb as the painting?"

"No, they are from separate tombs," said Daoud. He gestured that Jennifer should lead them back to the other room. Grandma Jo followed, but stayed well behind.

"Who was she?" asked Jennifer, looking down at the mummy.

"Alas, we do not know," said Daoud. "She was found, like so many others, in a cache of mummies, in an unmarked tomb. Mummies were often removed from their own tombs to save them from looting by grave robbers. We only know that she is from the Eighteenth Dynasty, and died sometime around 1500 B.C."

"That's, let's see, about thirty-five hundred years ago," said Jennifer, "right?"

"Absolutely right," said Daoud. "Do you know much about mummies?"

"I know they removed the mummies' liver, lungs,

stomach and intestines," said Jennifer. She nodded at a collection of four stone jars in a display case some distance away. "They kept them in jars like those."

"The canopic jars, yes. The heart, the seat of memory and thought, however, they left in the body cavity," said Daoud.

"But they pulled the brains out through the noses and threw them away."

"They thought the brains weren't worth anything," Daoud said, with a smile.

"I know some people whose brains sure aren't," said Jennifer, thinking of Tyler and his annoying practical jokes.

"So do I," said Daoud, his eyes creasing. "So, tell me what came next, in the matter of mummification."

"Um. After that, they packed the body in natron, a kind of salt, and then let it dry out for seventy days."

"Quite correct. Then the mummy was wrapped in layers of linen and placed in its sarcophagus to begin the journey to the afterworld." Daoud grinned. "Pickled and packaged, I remember one tourist saying, all for the sake of immortality."

Jennifer laughed.

"You know your subject," said Daoud. "Do you want to become an Egyptologist?"

"I don't know." Jennifer shrugged. "I haven't really thought about it."

"Of course. Well, that is the extent of this traveling collection," said Daoud. "Wait a moment, though, please." He strode into the other room.

Jennifer went to stand by Grandma Jo, who was carefully not looking at the mummy.

"Where did Daoud go?" she asked.

"I don't know," said Jennifer. "He just said to wait. I wanted to ask him more about that tomb painting." Jennifer started to walk over to it, but Daoud returned, carrying a small cloth bag.

"For you," he said, pulling an intricate beaded necklace from the bag. He handed it to Grandma Jo.

"Oh, Daoud, you don't have to do that," said Grandma Jo, admiring the way the beads glittered in the light. "I have nothing for you…"

"Your presence is enough to brighten my day," said Daoud.

"Well…thank you," said Grandma Jo. "It's beautiful."

Daoud turned to Jennifer. "And for you." He laid a heavy, cool item in her hand.

Jennifer looked at it. "A scarab! Wow!"

The gold-flecked dark blue stone amulet just filled her palm. Lines cut into the top formed the outline of a head and wings. Along the edges, more scoring gave the impression of an insect's bent legs; and at the top of the scarab, a hole had been drilled so it could be worn as a pendant.

"Daoud, is that what I think it is?" asked Grandma Jo. "That's a family heirloom! I remember you showing it to me when we visited your house. You can't give it away."

"I have no children, and I am the last of my siblings." Daoud shrugged. "I am happy to give it to someone who will truly appreciate it."

"Thanks!" said Jennifer.

"Sacred to Ra, scarab amulets were thought to have mystical powers and be linked to the wearer's life force, or ka," said Daoud. "They were also said to be effective against demons."

"Demons?" Grandma Jo laughed.

"The ancient Egyptians were much concerned with them," Daoud explained.

"I'm sure it will help Jennifer with any she might encounter."

Daoud looked at his watch. "I would like to tell you more, but I have a meeting that I must attend. Perhaps when you return, we can talk again, Je…Jennifer."

With a brief bow, he was gone.

Grandma Jo shook her head. "He hasn't slowed down a bit. Harriet and I always had a hard time keeping up with him." She glanced at her own watch. "I guess we should go, too. I promised your mother I'd have you home by lunch."

Jennifer gave the tomb painting one last look on the way out. "I hope I find out more about that."

"I hope you do, too."

It had rained while they were in the museum. Grandma Jo retrieved her shapeless black bag from the coat check staff and pulled a folded umbrella out of it. Jennifer loved her bag; it always seemed to have more stuff and more room in it than was logically possible.

Grandma Jo's car was parked across the street.

Jennifer tried jumping a wide puddle, but missed, thoroughly soaking her feet. When she got into the car, she put the scarab on the dashboard, fastened her seatbelt, and took off her socks and shoes. Grandma Jo started the car and turned on the heat.

As she pulled away from the curb, the front tire dipped into a pothole. Jennifer grabbed the scarab before it could slide to the floor.

"I wish they'd fix these streets," Grandma Jo grumbled as she merged into traffic.

The cool stone of the scarab warmed in Jennifer's hands. It was dulled with age, but still beautiful. She flipped it over, to discover that the base was covered in hieroglyphs, tiny but precise. She thought some of them might be similar to the ones on the tomb painting.

Most hieroglyphs were basic sounds. Early Egyptologists had made their best guess at where the vowels were supposed to go, as hieroglyphs didn't indicate that.

"Ma," she said, tracing some that she recognized with her fingernail. "Ka. Re. Dje. Nefer. Huh."

"What?" asked Grandma Jo, concentrating on the traffic.

"Nothing," said Jennifer. "It's just that these sort of sounded like my name."

"That's nice," said Grandma Jo, swerving to avoid a dip in the road.

There were more hieroglyphs. Jennifer wet her finger and rubbed the moisture across the carvings to see them better. Three tiny ones marched down one side of the base. These had meanings, as well as sounds. The first was a pair of legs, which meant "to walk" or "to travel." Next, there was a shape like an "X." That meant "to separate" or "to break." And then there was a carving of a scarab.

To travel—somewhere—break the beetle? Did that mean, break the scarab itself?

Jennifer slouched in the seat and stared at the amulet. It had warmed up now, and felt almost hot to the touch. Perhaps the "X" meant "open," not "break." She turned it over, but didn't see any opening. Along the edge, though, where the lines that indicated the legs were scored, there seemed to be an extra line. It was so thin, she hadn't noticed it before. It went all the way around the amulet.

Jennifer wriggled a thumbnail into it. The line widened. Several tiny amber grains fell into her hand.

"What's that smell?" asked Grandma Jo, pulling ahead to pass the slow vehicle in front of her.

"My feet?" Jennifer suggested, wriggling her toes under the blast of warm air from the heater.

"No, it's sharp, and a little bitter, but pleasant."

"Can't be my feet, then," said Jennifer. She could smell it now, too. She lifted her hand and the scent increased. Was it coming from the scarab? She sniffed at it.

Grandma Jo chuckled, then frowned. "We're going to be late. Look at the time!"

"Time?"

"Yes—oh, no! Brace yourself!"

"What?"

The car hit another pothole. The amulet, which Jennifer held close to her face, popped open. She gasped as the lid swung back. Dust puffed out, filling her nose and mouth. As she breathed it in, she was struck with a sickening dizziness.

Her mind swirled—and was sucked down into a glittering, black velvet nothing.

Jennifer opened her eyes. Dust particles glimmered in the bright sunlight that poured in from a high, barred window.

For a moment, confusing images of a sparkling darkness, an insect and a man wearing a crown floated through her mind. Then they were gone, like the memory of a dream.

A heavy weight pressed down on her ribs. She lifted her head and peered blearily into a pair of bright yellow eyes.

"Mrr?" a skinny spotted cat with ears too large for its head had its forelegs braced on her chest. Jennifer blinked. The little cat hissed at her, then leaped away and skittered through an open doorway, as fast as its legs would take it.

Jennifer took a startled breath as the small room came into better focus. One of the walls was a woven brown curtain, but the other three were solid. All of them, including the curtain, were decorated with bright Egyptian-style drawings of plants, animals and people. The vivid colors glowed in the light from the window.

"Where am I?" Jennifer mumbled. Her mind felt fuzzy. She'd been at the museum, and…and what? There had been a mummy. That was all she could remember.

She struggled to sit upright, but her body didn't want to obey her. It didn't feel quite right. It was like wearing a shirt that was too tight in some places and too loose in others. Her arms trembled as she pushed against the mattress. At last, she managed to maneuver herself upright, with her back against the wall. Her legs, half-off the mattress, were tangled in a thin white sheet. In her struggle, she knocked over a crescent-shaped clay brick that had been at the head of her bed. She set it straight with a shaky hand—and froze.

The hand had dark brown skin. Both her hands were dark, with paler skin on the palms. She reached up to feel her face. Her nose and lips and ears felt the same, but there was something wrong with her hair. She pulled a long strand around in front of her eyes and stared at it. Her own hair was straight, a light brown. This stuff was thick, black and wavy. She tugged on it, hard.

"Ow!" she said at the sharp pain in her scalp. "Okay. Not a wig. This is weird." Her voice was hoarse.

Jennifer wobbled to her feet, holding the wall for support, and looked around. The only other items in the room were two red clay pots, polished smooth. The wooden floor creaked as she stumbled towards them. One of them held a collection of beads and fabric dolls. The other was empty, but she thought she could guess what it was for. She wrinkled her nose at the faint acrid smell.

With one hand still on the wall, Jennifer staggered through the doorway through which the little cat had run. It turned out to be a larger room, furnished with more items. A thick mattress covered a low bed, wider than her own. It had sturdy wooden legs and a raised lip at the bottom. It was tilted slightly upwards at the head, where two leather-covered crescent shapes rested. Beside the bed was a small, spindly-legged wooden table with one large drawer and a graceful low chair with a curved seat and wooden legs that ended in beast paws.

Another doorway led from the room into what looked like a garden. Jennifer glimpsed a bright blue sky and the flat sides of other buildings over a fence of tall, waving plants.

For a moment, her vision blurred, as though she was seeing through a lens that wasn't quite focused. Then it cleared again.

"Dje-Nefer?" someone called.

"Eep!" said Jennifer. She'd thought she was alone!

"Dje-Nefer, are you up?" It was a woman's voice. It seemed to be coming from the rooftop garden.

Jennifer crept through the door and looked around, but there was no one there.

"Dje-Nefer! Come and have your breakfast."

Jennifer padded down the narrow path, between the tall staked vegetables. There was a foot-high wall of bricks in the middle, outlining what looked to be a hole in the roof. Jennifer peered into it. A black-haired, dark-skinned woman smiled up at her from the floor below. Her eyes were outlined with thick black lines. It was no one Jennifer knew.

"Ah, there you are," she said. "Are you awake yet?"

"I'm not sure," said Jennifer.

The woman laughed. "Come eat, dear one. I let you sleep in today, but that's long enough."

"C-coming," said Jennifer. Her voice was hoarse.

She looked for stairs, but there weren't any on the rooftop. Jennifer returned through the doorway to the large room, then stopped and stared. The wall above and beside the door to the smaller room where she had awoken was covered in more bright paintings. A beautiful woman spread her protecting wings over the door, framing it on one side, while another woman with long curved horns on her head reached from the other. Isis and Hathor. Whoever had painted them was a wonderful artist.

Beside the door was another hole in the floor, like the one in the garden. Stairs jutted out from the wall, descending to the floor below. Jennifer braced one palm against the wall as she took the stairs one at a time, trying not to trip on the hem of her dress. The stairs led to a large room with a tiled floor that was cool under her feet. The room was dim, a small barred window like the one upstairs being the only source of light. She thought she could make out a few pieces of delicate furniture.

"Hurry up, please, Dje-Nefer," said the woman.

"How does she know my name?" Jennifer whispered. "Even if she is saying it wrong."

She followed the voice into another room, this one obviously a cooking area, though not like any kitchen that Jennifer had ever seen. There were no tables or counters, and the only furniture was a set of wooden shelves laden with pots and bowls. Thanks to the hole in the roof, this room was full of sunlight, illuminating the woman. She had pulled up the hem of her long white dress and was kneeling on the floor, rolling a smooth round rock on top of a flat stone that had been laid between the tiles. She looked up, and Jennifer realized who the model for Hathor had been.

"Here is your breakfast," she said, pointing to a small bowl and mug on a striped mat laid out on the floor. Jennifer sat. The bowl was full of a warm, grainy porridge, dotted with glossy black morsels. Jennifer sniffed. It didn't smell too bad, and she was hungry. She looked for a spoon, but there wasn't one. She opened her mouth to ask for one, but some inner caution told her not to. Shrugging, she dipped her fingers into the bowl and scooped some of the mush into her mouth.

Jennifer's eyebrows rose in appreciation. The black bits turned out to be sweet and juicy, the grains crunchy and tart. She ate it all, then reached for the mug. Spicy, hot tea cleared her mouth and her mind.

Beside her, the woman lifted some grains out of a clay pot and sprinkled them on the flat stone. Jennifer watched her roll the rock over the grains, crushing them in quick, practiced strokes.

"Finished?" the woman asked. "Good, you can help me with the bread then."

The woman now had a respectable pile of fine brown powder, ground from the grains. She scooped it up with both hands and poured it into a terra cotta bowl. After making a small indentation in the center of the powder, she dribbled a bit of liquid into the bowl from a small pot decorated with a hippopotamus on the lid.

"Here, knead this for me while I stoke up the fire," she said, handing the bowl to Jennifer.

The dough inside was sticky and smelled of yeast. Jennifer rolled and punched the dough, using her shoulders the way Grandma Jo had taught her. She stopped, her eyes widening. Grandma Jo—was she here, too? Wherever 'here' was. Grandma Jo had been with her when…Jennifer frowned, then shook her head. She couldn't remember.

"What's wrong?" asked the woman.

"Uh," said Jennifer. "Nothing." She started kneading again.

The kitchen, already quite warm, was getting hotter as the woman raked up coals in a brick-lined fireplace in a corner of the room. When the coals were bright red, she wedged two round-bottomed clay pots well into the pile.

"Done?" she asked Jennifer. "Good job. We'll let it rise while the ovens heat up."

Jennifer nodded. The woman gave her a puzzled look.

"You're awfully quiet this morning," she said.

"Uh, just tired, I guess," said Jennifer.

The woman laughed as she covered the dough with a cloth. "I'm not surprised. You were up very late last night, watching the sky-goddess. Ramose found you asleep in the garden, with only Nut's stars for company, and carried you to your bed. You didn't wake even when Mentmose got up this morning."

"Oh," said Jennifer, wondering who Ramose and Mentmose were.

"Now pick up your dishes, dear, and put them in the washing bowl." The woman pointed vaguely at a corner

26

of the room where several large bowls rested on the floor. "Don't forget to pour some water over them this time, or they will dry. You remember how hard you had to scrub yesterday."

Jennifer carried her dishes to the corner and peeked in each bowl. One of them already had mugs and bowls in it, soaking in water. She dutifully scooped up some of the dirty water with her mug and poured it in her bowl, then put both items in with the rest.

"We'll have to get more water today," said the woman. "Our jug is nearly empty."

A tall teenage boy, wearing only a dusty, stained kilt flung himself into the room. His chest was bare, except for a necklace of red and black beads. He grinned when he saw Jennifer.

"About time you were up, minnow," he said. His black hair was almost as long as Jennifer's, but it was tied back in a ponytail. The lines around his eyes were smudged. "I wish I could get away with sleeping in."

"Mentmose, you are fifteen now, and since you insist that you are a man, you must also hold to a man's work and a man's hours," said the woman. "If Ramose rises early, then so must you."

Mentmose grimaced. "I know." But his smiled returned quickly. "The minnow will have to hold to a woman's hours soon enough."

"She is not yet fourteen, nor is she betrothed, as you are."

Mentmose grunted and rolled his eyes.

"Was there something you wanted?" the woman asked.

"Oh! Yes. Father asks me to ask you to buy him some polishing powder next time you go to the market."

"Why? He usually does that himself," the woman protested.

"I do," said a man who came striding through the doorway. He was dressed almost identically to Mentmose, except that his kilt was cleaner and his eye makeup tidy. "But I have a commission to complete as soon as possible. And Meryt-Re, you are so much better than I at charming old Hapu. He is sure to give you a lower price than he does for me."

The woman—Meryt-Re—chuckled. "Flatterer. All right, husband, I will do your shopping for you."

"Thank you. Oh—has my brother come by yet?" asked her husband. "He said he was going to."

"No, Ramose," Meryt-Re began. She stopped, as they all heard a knock. "That may be him."

"I'll check," said Ramose, and left the room. A moment later, he returned, another man beside him.

Jennifer blinked in surprise. She had expected to see someone just like Ramose, but this man was completely hairless, except for his eyebrows, which, she realized, were only painted on. Like the others, his eyes were outlined by thick black makeup, but his extended in two lines halfway to his ears. His white, intricately-pleated kilt was spotless. The skin of a leopard was tied over one shoulder, its head and large paws flopping down his bare chest. He stood taller than Ramose, but had the same general features, though his were composed in an expression of great gravity.

"Good morning, Neferhotep," said Meryt-Re, smiling at him.

"Good morning," he said, his voice and face solemn.

"Have they given you some time off from your temple duties today?" asked Meryt-Re.

"A little time," said Neferhotep. "Enough to visit my family, at least."

"Wonderful. We don't see you often enough, now that you've become a priest of Amon-Ra," said Meryt-Re. "Would you like something to eat?"

Neferhotep grinned, suddenly looking younger. "Your cooking is better than any at the temple, Meryt-Re," he said. "I would be delighted, if it's not too much trouble."

Meryt-Re laughed. "Dje-Nefer just finished her breakfast. There is still some in the pot."

"So, is this the reason you asked to visit today?" asked Ramose, smiling. "So you could cadge a meal?"

Neferhotep blushed, his dark skin turning a reddish-brown. "Of course not."

"No?" asked Meryt-Re, her brows rising.

"Well…yes. But I also came to ask if you would be able to provide me with some more of your work, Ramose. My superior, Ka-Aper, liked the pieces I showed him. He asked where I had gotten them, and wanted to know if there were more."

"Ka-Aper? The sem priest?" asked Ramose.

"Yes. As a priest of the first rank, he performs most

of the Opening of the Mouth ceremonies for noble mummies," said Neferhotep.

Mentmose whistled.

"Father—to have a sem priest request our amulets," he said, his eyes shining.

"And does it not count that I request them all the time?" asked Neferhotep, with a solemn face, but with a twinkle in his eye.

"Well, yes, but you're just Uncle Neferhotep," said Mentmose.

"And also a newly-minted priest of Amon-Ra," said Ramose, with a frown at his son, "and therefore deserving of your respect." He turned to Neferhotep. "When does Ka-Aper want to see my work? I can bring some pieces to the temple."

Neferhotep winced. "Well, that's the other reason I came by. I told him he could join us for dinner. Here."

"Here? When?" said Meryt-Re, handing him a bowl.

"Um. Tonight," he said, sniffing appreciatively.

"Tonight!" said Meryt-Re, her eyes widening. "Well, I suppose. But I'll have to buy some food. I don't really have the right ingredients for a meal with such a noble guest."

"I can give you a temple papyrus for use at the market," said Neferhotep, around a mouthful of porridge. "It would entitle you to any goods you may wish to use it for."

"That would help," said Meryt-Re. "I could also trade some of the barley cakes I baked this morning. Oh, Neferhotep, must it be tonight?"

He nodded. "It was the only time Ka-Aper had free." Neferhotep handed her the empty bowl.

"I just don't know," said Meryt-Re.

"It could advance Ramose's career. And mine, frankly. I told him how good a cook you are, but I don't think he believed me. You could prove it to him."

"Oh, all right," said Meryt-Re, absently passing the bowl to Jennifer.

"Tell him we would be honored," said Ramose, standing straighter.

"Excellent!" said Neferhotep. "Thank you."

Meryt-Re waved this off, frowning. "We'll have to go to the market as soon as possible, then, if I am to shop. It is later than I like. All the best items will already be gone."

Jennifer took Neferhotep's empty dish to the washing bowl, remembering to pour water into it, though it hardly needed cleaning. Neferhotep had wiped it bare.

"I wonder what I should make," said Meryt-Re.

"How about duck?" suggested Ramose, his voice hopeful.

Meryt-Re smiled at him. "I know how you love them, Ramose, but it may not be possible. Meat like that has been scarce lately."

"Because of the drought, I know," said Ramose, sighing. "Everything is getting scarce."

"The Pharaoh is very concerned about it," said Neferhotep.

"No doubt," said Meryt-Re, with a slight grimace. "Well. Our bread should be risen by the time we return from shopping. I can bake it then. Come, Dje-Nefer."

"M-me?" said Jennifer, startled.

"Of course," said Meryt-Re. "I'll need your help carrying the baskets." She gestured at a stack of them in one corner of the room.

"I need to go, too," said Neferhotep. "We are meeting with Parahotep today to discuss his funerary rites. He is almost at his life's end. The doctors can do nothing for him."

"Is he the one who wants to preserve his brain?" asked Mentmose, smirking.

"Yes," said Neferhotep, shaking his head. "He has a theory that the brain has a use. Well, at least he is willing to concede that the other organs are more important." He dug in a pouch that hung from the thin leather strap over his shoulder and handed a small roll of papyrus to Meryt-Re. "Here is a temple chit. It will entitle you to a measure of food."

"Thank you," said Meryt-Re, unrolling it. The papyrus was crammed with hieroglyphs. "Are you sure it says what it is supposed to say?"

"It is my own work," said Neferhotep, with a lift of his chin.

"It's very nice," she assured him.

"And I almost forgot this, too," said Neferhotep. "My apologies."

He pulled something from underneath his leopard skin and gave it to Ramose.

"Ah, yes," said Ramose. "You showed it to Ka-Aper?"

"Yes. It's why he wanted to see more. He asked if he could keep it, since it is a sign sacred to Amon-Ra, but I had to tell him no."

"As well," said Ramose. "I made this for a very special young lady. I was going to wait for your birth anniversary." He glanced at Meryt-Re, who rolled her eyes.

"Oh, all right," she said, "but please be quick about it."

"Can you guess who this is for?" asked Ramose, smiling at Jennifer.

She shook her head, bewildered.

"For my beautiful daughter," said Ramose. He allowed the item to fall from his hand, where it dangled, spinning in the sunlight.

Jennifer gasped. The amulet!

The scarab amulet! Jennifer's memory flooded back. Grandma Jo—the museum—the tomb painting—the hieroglyphs—the dust inside the amulet, blowing into her face…and the dizzying tumble through the sparkling darkness. Then waking up to find herself…here.

In…

In ancient Egypt.

The amulet had caused her to travel through time.

Jennifer swayed, nearly falling.

"Are you all right?" asked Meryt-Re, steadying her with one hand.

"I'm, uh, fine," said Jennifer.

"Just tired, I imagine," said Ramose, smiling fondly at her. "I had to carry her in from the garden last night," he told Neferhotep. "She was fast asleep, with her head in the herbs. I couldn't even wake her."

"Truly?" asked Neferhotep. Jennifer glanced at him. He was staring at her with an odd expression. "Were you stargazing again last night?"

"Uh, yes," she said, remembering what Meryt-Re

had mentioned earlier.

"It's all right, Neferhotep," said Meryt-Re. "You know she's been doing that since she was three years old. Nothing bad has ever happened."

"I know," said Neferhotep, sighing. "But I do worry. The Walkers of the Night. . ."

Ramose laughed. "The demons? Oh, Neferhotep."

"They do exist," said Neferhotep, solemnly.

"Well, we've never had a problem. Besides, you put protective spells around the garden years ago, and you renew them every year. Nothing could get in."

"I suppose. And Miw would warn you if one did. It's time I renewed those spells, though."

"As you wish," said Ramose.

"We would appreciate that," said Meryt-Re, with a glance at her husband. "We appreciate everything you do for us. Not everyone has a priest of Amon-Ra in the family."

Neferhotep shrugged.

"If you are truly worried, then perhaps this will help," said Ramose, lifting the amulet. He lowered the thong over Jennifer's head, and it settled in front of her chest with a comforting weight. She had recognized it instantly, though in this time it was still bright and clean. She gripped it in her fist. It felt right, like something she had been meant to wear.

"Thank you," she said to Ramose.

"And look," he said. "It is not just a heart scarab." He gestured for her to let go of the amulet. "Do you see the latch? Ah, my clever child. You open it like you already knew how."

Jennifer pried the amulet open a little way. She hesitated, then held her breath and pulled it apart.

"See?" said Ramose. "It is hollow."

Jennifer let her breath trickle out. It was empty. She hadn't been sure what would happen when the amulet opened. She ran a finger around the inside, which had been polished smooth.

What had Grandma Jo thought, when she disappeared? Or—maybe she hadn't.

They were calling her 'Dje-Nefer,' and they didn't seem surprised to see her. Maybe, when she traveled through time, she had somehow ended up in someone else's body—Dje-Nefer's. This body had different skin and hair…perhaps it wasn't her own. She remembered how she had felt when she woke up.

That meant Dje-Nefer could be in her body, back in her own time. She shook her head. No. Forward in her own time. Jennifer shivered, feeling the long black hair brush her shoulders.

"What's the matter, Dje-Nefer?" asked Meryt-Re.

Jennifer looked at her, then at the others. Ramose was still smiling at her. Neferhotep's eyes narrowed, as he watched her.

Should she tell them? That she had traveled through time, and wasn't really Dje-Nefer? She doubted they would believe her. She wasn't sure she entirely believed it herself.

No. They would laugh. They might even think she was some sort of demon, like this Neferhotep fellow was so worried about.

She gave them a weak smile. "Just tired, like you said."

"Did you dream?" Neferhotep asked abruptly.

"Uh…yes," said Jennifer, startled into remembering. "There was a man…I think…with a white, uh, crown.

39

Split into two sections."

Neferhotep's painted eyebrows shot up. "Amon-Ra!"

"There, you see," said Ramose. "Nothing to worry about. If Amon-Ra is coming to my daughter in her dreams, then she is well-protected. He and this scarab will keep her safe."

"Well…that is so," said Neferhotep. Now he looked at Jennifer with an entirely different expression. Thoughtful, even respectful. "Dreams are powerful omens, you know."

"That's true," said Meryt-Re, "but if you wish to discuss this any further with Dje-Nefer, it will have to wait, Neferhotep. We must get to the market."

"Yes, of course," said Neferhotep. "I didn't mean to delay you. But, if you don't mind—I'd like to offer more protection for your daughter, in the form of a spell. Will you allow me to do that?"

"Certainly," said Meryt-Re.

"Good. It may take me some weeks to concoct, however," said Neferhotep. "I will go and return at sunset, with Ka-Aper. May Amon-Ra watch over you all."

He bowed and left the kitchen. Ramose followed,

then came back alone.

"Now," said Meryt-Re, business-like, "we must get going. Mentmose, I need you to go to the river and fill the water jar."

Mentmose scowled. "But father was going to show me how to make tjehnet today."

"It will have to wait. I will probably need your help this afternoon to do the cooking, too."

"But," said Mentmose. "Oh, all right."

Ramose clapped him on the shoulder. "We would need more water to make the paste anyway. Help your mother today. We can grind the turquoise and the clay for the tjehnet tomorrow. Besides, it might be wise for you to learn some cooking skills."

"That's for girls," scoffed Mentmose.

"Yes, but it is still worth learning," said Ramose. "Now I must be off to my workshop to choose which pieces I should present to the honorable Ka-Aper."

Mentmose sighed. Hefting the water jug onto his hip, he headed for the doorway.

"I think we'll take two baskets," said Meryt-Re. "I'll carry one and you can carry the other, Dje-Nefer."

41

She plucked two woven baskets out of the pile, one of which she had slung over her arm. She handed the other to Jennifer. Meryt-Re rummaged on the shelves and proceeded to fill her basket with several flat round pastries that looked something like cinnamon buns.

"There. We can go now," said Meryt-Re. "Oh, wait—why haven't you put any kohl on your eyes yet? Oh, never mind. I'll get some."

She left, and Jennifer could hear her trotting up the stairs. It was only a minute before she was back, carrying a small clay pot and a brush. With quick, expert strokes, she outlined Jennifer's eyes with a sticky black paint. It dried instantly, but itched. Jennifer had to stop herself from rubbing at it.

"Don't you smudge that," said Meryt-Re, holding up a warning hand. "All right, let's go."

She picked up her basket, and Jennifer followed her into the larger room, which had a wide wooden door set into one wall. As she opened it, a blast of noise from the street poured into the room.

People streamed past in both directions. Most of them wore Egyptian-style outfits like Ramose and

Meryt-Re, but there were also men and women wearing baggy tunics and head scarves, or outfits of gaudy fabric wrapped around their bodies, or short woolen kilts and vests. Some even wore shining helmets and pieces of armor. A group of children ran by, all of them naked. The boys' heads were shaved bald, except for one long lock that dangled from the right side.

As she and Meryt-Re stepped outside, Jennifer blinked in the bright sunlight. It nearly blinded her after the cool darkness of the house.

The sweat that trickled down Jennifer's sides in the intense heat dried almost as soon as it formed, too quickly to wet the fabric of the dress. She thought she now understood why the ancient Egyptians wore such loose, light clothing, and briefly envied the naked children. She licked dry lips, feeling like she was turning into a mummy on the spot.

Jennifer tried to keep up with Meryt-Re's purposeful strides. Her bare feet slapped the paved road, sending up tiny puffs of dust from between the stones. Sand filled the cracks and mounded up in miniature dunes against the edges of the tall buildings surrounding them.

The buildings were covered from top to bottom in hieroglyphs and brightly-painted reliefs of people, animals and gods. They weren't as nice as the ones inside Dje-Nefer's house, she decided.

On one building, a giant mural of a god with the head of a bird dominated the wall. The bird's beak curved gracefully downwards, and he held a scroll in one open hand. From a door near the base, a man wearing a white kilt and a thin leather strap that lay diagonally across his chest led a single file of identically dressed boys of different ages away down the street. Jennifer realized that the bird-headed god must be Thoth, the patron of scribes, and that the building had to be a school.

Jennifer frowned. "Shouldn't I be in school, too?" she asked.

Meryt-Re groaned. "You're not going to start that again, are you? Mentmose had his few years, but I thought we established long ago that girls do not go to school, Dje-Nefer." Meryt-Re threw Jennifer an exasperated look. "No matter how much they nag their mothers."

"Sorry," Jennifer mumbled.

Meryt-Re shook her head and strode away. Jennifer hurried to catch up with her. Hundreds of people filled the street, some strolling, others walking more quickly, although no one was foolish enough to run in the relentless heat. Meryt-Re threaded herself easily through the crowd. Jennifer tried to stay as close as possible to her. Once, Meryt-Re grabbed her arm to pull her closer, and they both ended up squeezed against the side of a building as four men carrying a richly-decorated sedan chair trotted by. A man wearing a striped headcloth sat regally under the canopy, looking bored. Jennifer couldn't help staring after him. Meryt-Re gently towed her away.

The market, which they reached in a remarkably short time, was even more crowded than the street. People here, however, were in no hurry. They meandered from booth to booth, stopping to chat with the vendors, to inspect the goods, and to buy. Jennifer gaped at the number and variety of items for sale. It was a riot of noise and color.

Bright awnings shaded untidy piles of ceramic pots at one booth and precise stacks of bronze plates at another. Across from them, mounds of baskets gave way to heaps of clay oil lamps. Further away, fabric pinned on a striped awning fought for space beside complete outfits, their beads sparkling in the sun, while long poles laid horizontally across tables dripped with glittering jewelry. And all around was noise, the sound of people talking, laughing, arguing, shouting, and even singing.

The market was a maze. Instead of being lined up in neat rows, the booths were spread out in no particular order, as if it had just grown there, like some strange garden. Meryt-Re seemed to know exactly where she was going, though. They twisted and turned, going first one way, then the other, swerving around a clump of jumbled booths, only to go back in almost the same direction they had come from. Meryt-Re walked steadily onwards, ignoring the shouts of the vendors, who held items out to her. Jennifer jogged beside her, staying close.

At last, Meryt-Re stopped at a tent held up at the four corners by long poles that slanted outwards, stretching the striped fabric taut. The awning shaded dozens of woven baskets, and a skinny man who sat cross-legged in the middle. Jennifer wrinkled her nose at the smell rising from the baskets. Flies bigger than she had ever seen in her life buzzed around, swooping in and out of the tent. Waving them away, she peered into one of the baskets. A few glassy-eyed fish stared back at her.

"Good morning, Seneb," said Meryt-Re. "What do you have today?"

"Finest catfish and perch," said Seneb, smiling at her. He was missing several teeth, Jennifer noticed. "I just caught them this morning."

Jennifer doubted that. Maybe it was the heat, but the fish sure smelled like they'd been out of the water longer than Seneb claimed. And frankly, he needed a bath, too. Jennifer breathed through her mouth as he lifted an arm and waved it at his stock.

"You won't find better anywhere else," he claimed.

Despite the heat and the fishy reek, Meryt-Re took her time examining the fish, inspecting each part, perhaps trying to find one that was actually fresh. Finally, she chose one that didn't look too bad, and picked it up, sliding her fingers under its gills.

"Will you take one of my barley cakes for this?" she asked.

"Your barley cakes are among the finest in the city,

47

Meryt-Re. But only one?" Seneb put his hand over his heart and arranged his face into a sad expression. "Dear lady, you wound me."

"It is not a very big fish, Seneb," said Meryt-Re. "I have seen far larger ones at your booth in the past."

"Alas, they are no longer to be found. It is the drought," said Seneb. "It has made everything scarce. Even the fish have deserted us for more hospitable areas. I assure you, these fine specimens were caught with considerable effort on my part. I cannot let them go for less than five cakes each."

"If, by effort, you mean that half the night you were lazing on your boat while your nets drifted in the river, I believe you," said Meryt-Re. "You are only trying to get as many of my cakes as you can. Two."

"It is the god's own truth that these perch are worth the gold found in the tombs of the pharaohs. Four cakes."

Meryt-Re pursed her lips, then sighed dramatically as she laid the fish back in its basket. "Well, if that is the way it is to be, I will have to look elsewhere." She turned to go.

"Wait! Wait, Meryt-Re," said Seneb, as he reached behind himself, digging in a small basket at his back. He showed a slightly larger, fresher-looking fish to Meryt-Re.

"Saving the best for yourself, Seneb?" she asked.

"Had you but asked, I would have offered it earlier," he said in an oily voice.

"Hm," said Meryt-Re. "Well, that is certainly better quality. I'll take it."

Seneb held it back as she reached for it. "Three cakes," he said.

Meryt-Re grimaced, then nodded. "Done." Seneb passed the fish to her. "Dje-Nefer?"

"What?" said Jennifer.

"Take the fish," said Meryt-Re.

"Oh. Right," said Jennifer. She slid two fingers under the gills, as she had seen Meryt-Re do, grimacing at the slimy feel, and almost dropped it. It landed in her basket with a plop. Jennifer wiggled her dirty fingers and wondered where to wipe them. Not her dress—it would smell bad all day. She finally settled on using a corner of Seneb's tent fabric.

Meanwhile, Meryt-Re had lifted her basket for Seneb to select his cakes. They were all the same, as far as Jennifer could see, but Seneb took his time to find the three biggest ones. Jennifer half-expected him to try to sneak another, but Meryt-Re was watching too closely.

Meryt-Re scowled and shook her head as they left Seneb's booth, but once out of his sight, her expression cleared.

"That old pirate. I could have gotten him down to two. But this is a very good fish, so I do not begrudge him the extra cake," said Meryt-Re. "I just hope Ka-Aper is satisfied with simple fare. As a high priest, he must be used to eating at the palace, and I doubt if they eat fish very often. Let us see if we can also find a duck. It has been a long time since your father tasted one."

Meryt-Re next headed towards a booth hung with the bodies of birds. Some were ducks, but other, smaller ones, were birds that Jennifer couldn't identify. They smelled bad, too, but not nearly as awful as Seneb and his fish.

Jennifer kept silent as Meryt-Re showed the papyrus that Neferhotep had given her to the bird vendor. After what seemed like a very heated argument, he finally accepted it and gave Meryt-Re a smallish duck in return. Meryt-Re dropped the duck into Jennifer's basket.

The bird-seller hung his head as they left, but when Jennifer glanced back, he was already smiling at his next customer.

A man pushed past her, and she stumbled, nearly dropping the basket. Meryt-Re pulled her away from him and his plodding donkey, both of them laden with clattering clay pots. Three short-legged, pointy-eared brown dogs yapped and bounced after him, nipping at the donkey's legs.

"Careful, Dje-Nefer," said Meryt-Re. "We made good bargains, but I don't have enough cakes, nor another of Neferhotep's papyri if we lost them. Come . . ."

"Dje-Nefer! Dje-Nefer!"

A young girl with frizzy black hair and a heart-shaped, delicate face came hurtling out of the crowd to fling one arm around Jennifer's neck. "Dje-Nefer! Your father said you would be here, and here you are. I'm so glad I found you. Do you like my new necklace? Mother says I can get new earrings, too. She's looking at some now. Oh! I love your scarab! Did your father make it? It's beautiful. I wish I had something like that. What did you get? Can I see? Oh, a duck! We had one last night, and it was bigger than this, but mother didn't like it. She says you just can't get good food right now. Are you having a special dinner?"

The girl paused for breath.

"Hello, Tetisheri," said Meryt-Re, slipping the words into the brief silence.

"Greetings of the day, Meryt-Re," said Tetisheri, bowing. She grinned at Jennifer, slipping her arm down around Jennifer's waist. "Will you be much longer? What else do you have to get?"

Jennifer opened her mouth to reply. She didn't want to say that she didn't know, but it didn't make any difference anyway. Tetisheri plowed on without waiting for an answer. Jennifer glanced at Meryt-Re, who was smiling and nodding, although she didn't really look like she was listening to the flood of words from Tetisheri.

"Isn't it late to be shopping?" asked Tetisheri, as usual, not waiting for an answer. "My mother sends our servants to shop for food in the morning, although she says she can't trust them to get the best. Look, a lot of the booths are closing for their afternoon naps. We should too. Always sleep when the sun is high, my mother says."

"I wish we could," said Meryt-Re. "No nap for us to-day. We have some cooking to do."

"Cooking! It will be so hot," said Tetisheri. "My mother always tells our cook to work in the mornings."

"We have no choice. The priest Ka-Aper is coming to dine with us this evening and we must prepare the meal," said Meryt-Re.

Tetisheri gasped. "Ka-Aper? Really? My father talks about him all the time."

"I suppose he would," said Meryt-Re. "Would you like to join us for the meal?"

Tetisheri squealed with delight. "Oh, may I? My parents are dining out tonight, and I will only have the servants as companions. Thank you!" And she dashed away, back in the direction she had come.

"We eat at sunset!" Meryt-Re shouted at her retreating back. Then she chuckled. "That girl. I am glad you and she get along so well. That will make it easier when she and Mentmose are married."

"Married!" said Jennifer, startled. Why, Tetisheri couldn't be much older than Jennifer!

"Oh, don't look so put out," said Meryt-Re. "You know they won't be wed for a few years yet. You still have time for girlish things." She looked speculatively at Jennifer. "But I suppose we ought to think of betrothing you again soon."

"Me?" said Jennifer, even more startled.

"Yes, you. It's such a shame that the boy we had chosen for you died when you were both toddlers. I remember you used to dress up in one of my old outfits and pretend you were getting married. You cried when we told you he had died of his sickness. He was such a nice boy. Ah, well. At least Mentmose's betrothed is healthy and pleasant. If a little chatty."

"Just a little," Jennifer muttered.

"We have a few more things to get," said Meryt-Re, "and, as Tetisheri reminded us, it is getting late."

Jennifer kept tight hold of her basket as they made their way down a winding path made by the food vendors, stopping here and there to buy small items. The bargaining for these went more swiftly, while Meryt-Re kept an eye on the sun. Soon, Jennifer had a chunk of soft white cheese, some small onions, a handful of almonds, a woven string of dates and a big cloth bag of beans in her basket, as well as the bag of polishing powder that Ramose had requested. Meryt-Re's supply of cakes steadily lowered. By far the most expensive item was a tiny pot of honey, which she bargained for with several of the cakes.

Meryt-Re stowed the honey carefully in her now-empty basket, and relieved Jennifer of some of her items. Jennifer was glad, for her basket was getting very heavy.

They wound their way back through the market, dodging other late shoppers intent on their own errands. The sun was high overhead when they left. Many of the vendors had shut their curtains or thrown sheets over their wares. Although the road was still crowded, most people, it seemed, deserted the streets when it got too hot. Jennifer could understand why. She hoped that Mentmose had been able to get the water jug filled, so she could have a drink.

A woman jostled Jennifer, and she gripped the

basket handle tighter. The woman mumbled an apology as she glanced over her shoulder and moved towards the side of the street. The rest of the people were also getting out of the way. Pinned up against the wall by the press of bodies, Jennifer could just barely see what had caused the commotion. Two armed men pushed people aside to clear space for a bald man wearing a leopard skin over one shoulder. The man's kilt had several complicated pleats and fell nearly to his ankles. He was walking under a striped canopy held up by four boys.

As he passed, some people bowed their heads in greeting, or perhaps salute. Jennifer wasn't sure which. The man ignored them.

But as he passed Jennifer, he glanced her way.

Even though she was almost melting in the heat, Jennifer shivered. For a brief moment, as their gazes met, she felt like a mouse being eyed by a snake.

"Dje-Nefer?" Meryt-Re called. "Oh, there you are."

"I'm coming," said Jennifer, tearing her gaze away from the striped canopy. "Sorry."

Who had that man been? She couldn't resist taking one last peek, but he was gone. She could just see the heels of one of the boys disappearing around a corner.

"Come on," said Meryt-Re, leading her back into the middle of the street. Jennifer looked up at the buildings they were passing. They didn't seem to be the same ones they had passed on the way to the market. Perhaps Meryt-Re had decided to take a different route home.

Meryt-Re led her around some tall stone columns, their every surface covered with hieroglyphs. Carvings in the stone were painted with bright blues, reds, and oranges. Jennifer stared up and up, to the very tops of the columns, which were capped with rounded blocks. Beyond them, a bird circled high above in the cloudless blue sky. Jennifer's eyes watered in the glare from the sun.

"Whatever are you gawking at, Dje-Nefer?" asked Meryt-Re. "You act like you've never seen these before."

Jennifer's head snapped down. "I, uh, thought I saw a hawk."

"A hawk? That's a good omen," said Meryt-Re. "Come along now, and mind you don't stumble. There are rough stones here."

Meryt-re turned a corner, and Jennifer dutifully followed, her gaze focused on the ground. She raised her eyes for a moment and stopped dead.

Before them was a ribbon of shining dark water, glittering in the sun. A wide stretch of black mud led down to it on either side. On the far bank, a few palm trees dotted the edge. Beyond that, the desert spread out over the land, rising in high, soft dunes of pinkish-brown sand. Farther away, the dunes flowed up against walls of craggy ivory stone that jutted into the sky.

"Great Hapi must be very sad," said Meryt-Re, shaking her head. "The Nile is so low."

The Nile! Jennifer grinned. The source of life and water for all of Egypt.

"I have never seen the river so depleted," Meryt-Re continued. "The canals are down to a mere trickle. Look, you can see it has gotten even lower since just a week ago. The nilometer isn't even in the water anymore."

Nearby, a man was cursing and struggling to push his reed boat away from the shore, where it was stuck fast. He swore again as he bumped against a spindly wooden structure with a sling tied to one end of a long pole. The sling lay flat on the ground, well away from the water.

Meryt-Re was eyeing it, too. "It will be harder to get water without the use of the shaduf," she said. Her voice lowered. "Seven years, we've had this drought. The Nile's annual flood has been sickly, hardly raising the level at all. I fear that not just Hapi, but perhaps all the gods, are not pleased with our Pharaoh, may Ma'at guide her soul."

Jennifer's head came up.

"Her?" she blurted. "Pharaoh" meant King, never Queen. All the Pharaohs had been male—except one. Could it be?

"Yes," said Meryt-Re, giving Jennifer a small frown. "Her Majesty Hatshepsut must surely be worried. The drought has all but emptied our country's grain storehouses."

59

Jennifer nodded, and tried not to smile. Hatshepsut! The famous female Pharaoh. She had taken the throne after her half-brother, Thutmose II, had died when his only son was just a baby. Despite the fact that only men could call themselves Pharaohs, she had taken the title. If the stories could be believed, she had even worn men's clothing and a Pharaoh's false beard.

Meryt-Re suddenly grabbed Jennifer and ran to the side of the road. Jennifer peered around her trying to see what was coming this time. Another sedan chair? She glanced at Meryt-Re, who stood rigid beside her, her lips compressed into a thin line, although her face was carefully blank.

A group of about twenty men wearing brilliant white kilts and shiny bronze helmets marched by. Their leader glowered at Jennifer and Meryt-Re as he shouted out the rhythm. Some of the men carried short swords and large painted shields; others had bows and quivers full of arrows slung over their shoulders. They passed in a jingle of weapons and the slap of sandals on the stones. Behind them, a man and a woman, their hands tied, stumbled along at the end of a rope. One of the soldiers tugged on it, making the woman cry out in pain as the rope dug into her wrists.

Meryt-Re watched them pass in silence. When they had all gone around the corner, she let out a long breath. "Pharaoh's soldiers," she said.

"Who were the people behind them?" asked Jennifer.

Meryt-Re bit her lip and glanced furtively around. She answered in a quiet voice. "Probably more so-called 'traitors' to the crown. There have been rather a lot of them lately. I must remember to watch what I say."

"You mean like about the drought?" asked Jennifer.

"Ssh!" said Meryt-Re. "We will speak no more of it." She walked away, basket swinging. Jennifer hurried to catch up.

Hatshepsut's restored temple had been decorated with paintings of trips to foreign lands, rather than battle scenes, like so many of the male Pharaohs had on theirs. Hatshepsut's reign had been peaceful, more concerned with trading ventures and the creation of beautiful monuments. Nothing indicated that she had needed soldiers to help enforce her reign.

Meryt-Re didn't talk again all the way back to the

house. Jennifer followed her through the front door and blinked in the sudden darkness, a relief after the sunlight outside. The tiles on the floor were deliciously cool against her sore, hot feet as she padded across the room behind Meryt-Re, and into the kitchen.

"Bes protect us," said Meryt-Re with a weary sigh. She patted the head of a small statue of a chubby dwarf, whose tongue stuck out from between his curly beard and moustache, as she passed by the kitchen shelving. "Let's hope he will make sure this evening's dinner impresses our guest, eh, little one?"

Jennifer nodded. Meryt-Re had swung her basket to the floor and was busy emptying it.

"Dje-Nefer, please check the dough. It should have risen by now," she said.

Jennifer looked under the cloth. The dough was twice the size it had been. "I think so," she said.

Meryt-Re took the bowl and punched the bread down again with her fists. Then she divided it in half and put both pieces on the floor, covering them again with the cloth.

"All right," she said. "Now we can pause for a bite to

eat. Are you hungry?"

Jennifer's stomach growled, and they both laughed. It had been a long time since breakfast.

"Did I hear someone mention a mid-day meal?" Ramose appeared around the corner of the kitchen, followed by Mentmose.

"No, you did not," said Meryt-Re, smiling, "but you shall have one, nonetheless. We can eat some of the cakes that I didn't take with me this morning and some cheese and dates, but that's all. The rest I need for this evening."

"I look forward to that," said Ramose. "Did you—"

"Yes, Ramose, I bought a duck. Not the best of birds perhaps, but it will serve."

"In your hands, it will dazzle," Ramose said.

Meryt-Re rolled out the eating mat, then rapidly laid food out on a plate. She set it in the middle of the mat, along with a clay jug and four mugs. All of them sat cross-legged around it, on the floor.

The liquid that Meryt-Re poured from the jug sparkled golden as it frothed into the mugs. Thirsty, Jennifer grabbed her mug and took a big gulp, then choked and almost spit it out. Too late, she remembered that beer was the common drink of the Egyptian people.

"Has it gone bad?" asked Meryt-Re, sniffing her own. She took a sip. "It seems all right to me."

Jennifer swallowed, wincing at the taste. "No, it's fine," she said, her voice hoarse. "Fine. I just…took too much."

"Drink up," said Ramose. "It's good for you."

Jennifer eyed him. He seemed perfectly serious. Thick and rich, the beer smelled a lot like the rising bread. All the same, she didn't think she would have any more. Feeling a little dizzy, she set the mug down.

The others had been busily stuffing themselves with the contents of the platter, especially Mentmose. Jennifer reached for a barley cake and some of the white cheese that Meryt-Re had bought in the market. Her eyebrows rose as she bit into it. It was delicious. She snatched a second piece out from under Mentmose's hovering fingers.

"Hey!" he said. "You should have better manners, minnow."

"Speaking of manners," said Ramose. "I expect you both to be on your best behavior this evening."

"Of course, Father," said Mentmose.

"I invited Tetisheri to dine with us, as well," said Meryt-Re.

Mentmose groaned. "Oh, no. Why? She'll spoil everything."

"Mentmose, she is your betrothed. You will marry her in a few years, and you really ought to have a better attitude about it," said Meryt-Re. "I'm sure you will come to appreciate her."

Mentmose snorted.

"Your mother and I were betrothed when we were babies," said Ramose, giving Meryt-Re a fond look. "Neither of us knew what to expect, but our marriage has been good. Wonderful, in fact." He smiled at Meryt-Re, who smiled back. "Yours will be, too. Even if Tetisheri is a bit of a ninny."

"Ramose!" said Meryt-Re, as Mentmose choked up, laughing. "You shouldn't say such things about your future daughter-in-law."

"Well, he's right," said Mentmose.

From what she'd seen of Tetisheri, Jennifer could only agree.

"Nevertheless," said Meryt-Re. "Treat her politely

tonight."

"All right," said Mentmose, sighing.

Meryt-Re gathered up the empty plate and the mugs, including Jennifer's half-full one. "Did you want this?"

Jennifer shook her head. Meryt-Re shrugged, then poured it back in the jug.

"Now we must get to work on this meal," she said, wiping her hands on a cloth. "I'll need you to turn the spit for the duck, Mentmose. Mind you remember to turn it at a constant speed. We don't want burnt meat on one side and raw on the other. Dje-Nefer, you can prepare the vegetables."

At least that was something she knew how to do. Meryt-Re rummaged on the shelves and handed Jennifer a bronze knife.

The rest of the afternoon went by in a blur. Meryt-Re took the risen dough and threw it into the hot ceramic ovens she had wedged into the fire earlier. The dough began to sizzle even before she slapped lids on the pots. As Jennifer chopped a small mound of onions and white roots, Meryt-Re flitted from one task to another. First she plucked the duck, nearly burying herself in a blizzard of feathers. Then she gutted it neatly. Jennifer was glad she hadn't been stuck with that messy job. She cleaned the fish as well, which was even worse, in Jennifer's opinion. The fish guts that she threw into a clay pot stank up the whole kitchen, and Mentmose was sent scurrying upstairs with it. Jennifer spotted him through the hole in the kitchen roof, pouring the slimy mess into a lidded container in the garden.

When he returned, he was set to sliding the duck on a metal pole. He propped it in the middle of the fireplace on two tall tripods.

"Grind this for me," said Meryt-Re, handing Jennifer some grains. She copied what she had seen Meryt-Re do earlier. Hers wasn't as fine as Meryt-Re's had been, but the woman seemed satisfied enough with the result.

As Mentmose turned the spit, grease from the duck spattered on the coals, sending clouds of gray smoke up through the skylight. While Meryt-Re filled the fish with a mixture of green herbs and patted Jennifer's crumbly flour on the outside, she had Jennifer turn the bread pots in the fire with a wooden paddle. Occasionally, Jennifer took a turn at the spit while Mentmose rested his arms.

Meryt-Re threw the chopped onions and a few of the roots into a metal pan, along with a bit of grease from the duck. The mouth-watering scent of frying onions filled the kitchen. Jennifer sniffed appreciatively.

"Smells good, doesn't it?" said Meryt-Re, smiling at her. "Now take the rest of those roots and add some oil and vinegar."

It took Jennifer a few moments to find those, but she eventually located them.

"Can I stop now, Mother?" asked Mentmose, rolling his shoulders.

Meryt-Re threw a double handful of almonds into the onion mixture and inspected the duck. Its skin was crispy and flaking.

"Yes, I think it is done," she said. "And just as well, for it is nearly time for our guests to arrive."

Jennifer glanced up at the skylight, surprised to see that the sun was lowering. She'd been so busy helping Meryt-Re that she hadn't noticed the time passing.

Mentmose let go of the spit with a groan and massaged his hands. Meryt-Re took the spit from Mentmose and expertly slid the duck off onto a pretty clay platter that Jennifer had found on the shelves. The fish, covered with the onion sauce, went onto another. Using the wooden paddle, Meryt-Re slid the bread out of the ovens. The crusts were burnt black, but Meryt-Re didn't seem dismayed by this. She deftly peeled them off with a sharp knife, leaving the inner cores steaming gently on a plate.

The last of the sunlight was just disappearing as they carried the dishes into the larger main room. Ramose was lighting several tiny clay oil lamps with a burning taper. Some he placed on the floor, and the others he hung from the ceiling. He had changed into a cleaner kilt.

"Ra goes to bed and Nut will soon watch over us," he said.

"May it always be so," said Meryt-Re. "Go change, Mentmose."

She turned to Jennifer and gestured that she should turn around. Jennifer did so, brushing at the front of her dress. A few crumbs fell, but she had managed not to spill anything on it. Meryt-Re nodded, satisfied.

"By Bes, that smells wonderful," said Ramose.

"You've outdone yourself, my dear."

"I only hope my humble efforts are enough," said Meryt-Re, twisting her hands together. "Oh, I'm so nervous, Ramose. What if he doesn't like it?"

Ramose put his arm around her shoulders. "I'm nervous, too," he admitted. "But we will show this Ka-Aper that we are capable of entertaining even the greatest of guests. Why, if the Pharaoh herself walked through our door, she would be impressed. Unless she has no taste."

"Ramose! You should not speak of her so," said Meryt-Re. "What if someone heard you?"

There was a knock on the door, startling them apart. Ramose opened it. Tetisheri stood in the doorway, bright-eyed and smiling. She wore a long white dress like Jennifer's, and gold earrings drooped from her ears, matching the necklace she had shown Jennifer in the market.

"Am I late?" she asked. "I wanted to come earlier, but first Father needed my help sorting his correspondence and then Mother wanted me to attend her when she went visiting, and then I had to change, and . . ."

"It's all right, Teti," said Meryt-Re. "Our guest will

be here shortly. But I should change, too. And get some scent balls for all of us!" She dashed up the stairs before Jennifer could puzzle out this reference, just as Mentmose was descending.

"Hello, Mentmose," said Tetisheri, her eyes shining.

He grunted in response. At a look from his father, he relented. "Hello, Tetisheri. That's a pretty outfit."

Tetisheri seemed to physically swell at this praise. She seized Mentmose in one hand and Jennifer in the other and towed them both into a corner, where she proceeded to tell them every detail of her trip to the market and to her mother's friend's house.

Jennifer glanced up at the window in the main room. Outside, the sky was darkening. The murmur of foot traffic seemed to have lessened considerably. She could hear voices, coming closer, although she couldn't make out what they were saying.

Meryt-Re dashed back down the stairs in a clean, white dress, a small bag swinging from one hand, just in time to hear a knock on their front door. Ramose swung it open and Neferhotep stepped inside, then gestured for his companion to follow. The man ducked under the sill and into the house, his face shadowed.

"Welcome, Ka-Aper, Reverend Sir," said Ramose, bowing. "We are honored by your presence."

"It is I who am honored," Ka-Aper said in a deep voice. He stepped into the light cast by the overhead oil lamps.

Jennifer took a step backwards. It was the man she had seen in the street, walking under the striped canopy.

The sun was long gone and the remains of their meal were laid out on the mat, reduced to nothing but crumbs and bones. Ka-Aper had eaten from the duck dish, but had only had a few bites of everything else except the fish, which both he and Neferhotep had refused. Neferhotep had murmured to Meryt-Re that they followed the ancient tradition of priests not eating fish. Meryt-Re had looked stricken, but Neferhotep apologized for not telling her earlier.

Most of the time, Ka-Aper had seemed polite and attentive, but every now and then, Jennifer thought she had seen the start of a faint and somehow superior smile on his face.

"You have lovely children," he said to Meryt-Re, scratching his chest under the wide pectoral necklace of alternating blue and gold beads. Several black scarabs hung within the beads, scattered all around the pectoral.

"Thank you," Meryt-Re murmured. She hadn't spoken much all evening, but she had watched everyone closely throughout and made sure their dishes remained filled.

None of the other family members had spoken much, either. But Tetisheri had chattered on, making up for all of them. Now she was watching Mentmose and Neferhotep play a game called 'Senet', which involved a carved wooden board, several polished stones and rules that Jennifer still hadn't figured out. Every time it was Mentmose's turn, Tetisheri made a suggestion. He rolled his eyes, but Jennifer noticed he usually did what Tetisheri said.

"You are fortunate to have a son," said Ka-Aper, sipping wine from a clay cup. He grimaced, then set the cup down. "Neferhotep says he bids fair to become a competent craftsman."

Meryt-Re lifted her chin. "He takes after his father."

"That's fortunate." Ka-Aper smiled. "And no doubt your daughter takes after you and will make a fine wife and hostess some day."

"If the gods will it," said Meryt-Re, with a slight flare to her nostrils.

"Neferhotep told me that Tetisheri will soon be

your daughter-in-law," said Ka-Aper. Jennifer thought she caught an edge of laughter in his voice.

Ramose cleared his throat. "So…Neferhotep said you wanted to see more of my work."

"Yes," said Ka-Aper, turning to him. "I was quite impressed with the pieces he showed me earlier. I was especially interested in the scarab that your daughter is wearing."

Jennifer wrapped her hand around it, hiding it from view.

"I carved it for her, especially," said Ramose. "I also included Amon-Ra's aspects as the god of wind and chaos, in prayers incised on the back."

"A princely item. It would be an appropriate gift for someone associated with Amon-Ra," said Ka-Aper.

"I could make another, similar to it," said Ramose. "As you can see, Dje-Nefer is already quite fond of this one."

"Hm, yes," said Ka-Aper, apparently losing interest in it. "Your work for Parahotep was very nice, too. Several of the other priests commented on the quality."

"Ptah guides my husband's hands," said Meryt-Re.

Ka-Aper inclined his head towards her. "So he must, since Ramose produces such fine work."

"Oh, sir?" said Neferhotep, laying a stone in place on the board. "I'm sorry, I forgot to tell you. Parahotep asked me after our meeting today if we could make sure his tomb is well-hidden."

Ka-Aper shook his head, smiling sadly. "They all do, Neferhotep. These are degenerate times. Tombs are robbed of their contents almost as soon as their inhabitants are laid to rest. Pharaoh Hatshepsut, blessings be upon her head, has tried many ways to stop these horrible desecrations, but they go on, nonetheless."

"The thieves are too sly, too experienced, for her soldiers," said Neferhotep. "They have been at it a long time. Whole families of thieves are often involved."

"How terrible!" said Meryt-Re.

Neferhotep nodded. "They take the offerings, the jewelry and amulets, the ushabti statues, and even the pottery. Sometimes they even take the canopic jars."

"Even the jars?" asked Meryt-Re. "But how are the people to function in the afterlife, with no internal organs? And then to have to work in the gods' fields with no little ushabti to take the burden from them."

"Do they sell the pieces?" asked Ramose, frowning.

"Upriver and down," said Neferhotep, placing a pebble on the board. "At least those in the tombs still have the Book of the Dead to guide them to the afterlife."

Tetisheri pointed to a spot on the senet board and whispered something to Mentmose.

"True," said Ka-Aper. He poured himself another cup of wine from an amphora, then replaced it in the clay ring that held it upright. "The robbers do not destroy the texts, for fear of Ma'at's judgment against them, I suppose, though I suspect that their hearts are already heavier than her sacred feather."

"May they be devoured by the monster of Osiris for their sins," Meryt-Re said in a low, fierce voice.

"Just so," said Ka-Aper. Jennifer thought she saw the ghost of a smile on his face.

"I regret to say some tombs are being defaced as well," Neferhotep added. "Names and images of the person are sometimes removed."

Meryt-Re gasped. "How are they to be remembered, then?"

"Some are not. Others have families which still retain some mementos," said Ka-Aper. "If only even a small image remains, then so does the memory."

"I do not like thieves," said Meryt-Re darkly.

"Well, Parahotep has created a truly devious system to keep himself safe," said Neferhotep. "He gave me the map of his proposed tomb."

"You had best hide it then, before anyone else sees it," said Ka-Aper.

"I will," said Neferhotep. "Carefully."

There was silence for a moment, broken only by the clack of pebbles on wood. Jennifer curled a lock of her long black hair around her finger. The marble-sized ball of oil and beeswax that Meryt-Re had pressed onto the top of her head had melted during dinner, releasing a flowery perfume. They had all worn them, although Neferhotep and Ka-Aper had refused, having brought their own scents.

Jennifer tried to hide a yawn behind her hand.

But Meryt-Re had seen it. "It is late," she said. "I think it is time for my children to go to bed. Tetisheri, I assume you will be staying the night?"

Tetisheri beamed at her. "I would be happy to."

"Very good. Mentmose, will you put a mattress down in Dje-Nefer's room for Teti, please?"

"Can't I do it later? I'm winning!" he protested.

"You can play some other time," said Meryt-Re.

"Leave the board as is, and next time we'll pick it up where we left off," suggested Neferhotep. "Unless your mother will let you stay up a little longer in the company of adults?"

"Oh, very well," said Meryt-Re, smiling at Mentmose. "Be quick about it, then."

"Yes!" said Mentmose, raising his hands in triumph.

"And Dje-Nefer—no star-gazing tonight, please," said Meryt-Re.

"Does your daughter have aspirations as an astronomer?" asked Ka-Aper, absently playing with his wine cup.

"She has always loved admiring Nut's beautiful jewelry," said Meryt-Re.

"She even fell asleep in the garden last night," Mentmose added.

"By the way, I checked the wards on the garden when I went upstairs this evening," said Neferhotep. "There is a spot where the reeds are bent down, perhaps from the weight of a bird landing. It may have affected the wards. I can renew them tomorrow, if you like."

"That would be fine," said Meryt-Re.

"Are you worried about the Walkers of the Night?" asked Ka-Aper, one corner of his mouth lifting. "Her amulet will protect her."

"Yes," said Neferhotep. Then he frowned at Jennifer. "But all the same, I suggest you stay indoors, Dje-Nefer."

"I am sure she will heed your good advice," said Ka-Aper.

"Come on, let's go," said Mentmose, picking up an oil lamp and rising. "I want to get back to the game."

"It was an honor to meet you, sir," said Tetisheri, as she curtseyed. Jennifer awkwardly copied her.

"I'm sure we will meet again sometime," said Ka-Aper, saluting them with his wine cup.

"Would you like to see my workshop now?" asked Ramose.

As the girls climbed the stairs, Jennifer glanced at him, sure she would find Ka-Aper watching her. His attention was all on Ramose.

"Yes, of course," said Ka-Aper. He followed Ramose and Neferhotep to the back of the main room. Meryt-Re was left to stack the dishes and carry them to the kitchen.

"Does your mother not have a servant yet?" asked Tetisheri.

"Uh…," said Jennifer.

"No," said Mentmose.

"Oh. Not even…"

"You know how she feels about slaves," said Mentmose, shaking his head.

"Yes," said Tetisheri, unusually terse.

Mentmose retrieved a mattress from his parents' room and unrolled it on the floor beside Jennifer's, then topped it with a thin blanket and a crescent-shaped headrest. Tetisheri's flow of chatter resumed as soon as he clattered down the stairs, taking the lamp with him.

Jennifer only half-listened to Tetisheri as the two girls got ready for bed. Meryt-Re had provided them all with toothpicks after the meal, but she longed for her toothbrush. She copied Tetisheri, who lay on her back on the mattress with her head nestled in the crescent-shaped brick. As she pulled up the sheet, Jennifer glanced out the high window. She wondered if Dje-Nefer missed her stars.

The little cat wandered into the room and stretched.

"Oh, there you are, Miw," said Tetisheri, patting her mattress, which the cat ignored. "Where have you been all evening? Do you think he likes me?"

"Who?" asked Jennifer, startled. "The cat?"

"No, silly! Mentmose," said Tetisheri.

"Oh. Um, sure."

Tetisheri heaved a great sigh. "I don't know. He just never seems very happy to see me. And I don't know what I'll do if he doesn't like me when we're married."

Jennifer was startled to see a tear on Tetisheri's cheek, glistening in the starlight. She tried to think of something comforting to say.

"I'm sure he'll come around. Boys are like that. My mother says they mature later than girls."

"Yes, that's true," said Tetisheri. "Even my mother says that." She wiped her face and was off again, babbling about what their house would look like when they were together. If it all came true, her dream home would have more furniture and ornaments than Jennifer could imagine. Finally, Tetisheri wound down, sort of like a car running out of gas. She drifted off to sleep right in the middle of a sentence.

Jennifer wriggled, trying to get comfortable on the silly headrest. Exasperated, she removed it completely and put her head down on the mattress. That was better, although she wished she had a pillow.

Tetisheri was already snoring gently, but despite the long, tiring day, Jennifer couldn't sleep. Trying not to wake the other girl, Jennifer crept from her bed into the other room. Meryt-Re's wide bed creaked as she sat on it and stared out the doorway into the garden. So many stars! She could understand Dje-Nefer's fascination. The only time Jennifer had seen so many was when she and her father had gone camping. Once, he'd taken his telescope and taught her the names of the constellations. She smiled, remembering, then swallowed. Would she ever see him or her mother again?

The sky looked different from the one at home. There was Orion the Hunter, down by the horizon, but sideways. Cassiopeia's 'W' was in the wrong place, too.

At least they were there, even if they weren't quite the way she remembered them. It was different here. Some of it strange, but some of it weirdly familiar. She felt…what was Grandma Jo's word for it?

"Discombobulated," she said. That was it. She felt discombobulated.

Jennifer hadn't removed the scarab necklace when she lay down. In the darkness, she couldn't see the hieroglyphs, but she could feel its smooth solidity. She hesitated, then flipped it open. It was still empty. She hadn't really expected it to suddenly fill with some sort of magical dust, but who knew? If she wanted to get back home, she would have to figure out what the dust was. She was sure the amulet and its dust must have had something to do with her coming to ancient Egypt.

She snapped the scarab closed again. A cool breeze brought the many scents of the garden into the room, some sweet, some spicy. Funny how it could be so hot during the day and so chilly now. She sniffed appreciatively at the fresh clean air. No brown ring of pollution here.

Jennifer lay back on the wide bed. Actually, she wasn't

sure she wanted to go home—not yet, anyway. Even though it was confusing and even exhausting at times, she was enjoying herself. It was cool to see the buildings with their bright paints still visible. The people were nice. Mostly. She wasn't sure she trusted Ka-Aper. Everyone else was fine. Tetisheri was too chatty but seemed a good friend to Dje-Nefer. Jennifer wondered what her own friends would think if they were here.

"Oh, they'd probably be bored," she said aloud. Or scared. Hannah wasn't interested in anything except clothes and makeup, and all Kelly and Ashley seemed to be able to talk about these days were boys and how immature that goof, Tyler, was acting. Jennifer felt like she was being left behind. She pretended to be interested in the same things, but really, it made for dull conversations. None of the others even wanted to play baseball any more. They'd all been together since the first grade, but now it was like they were drifting apart. All three of them had laughed at her when she'd made the mistake of being excited about the Egypt topics.

Jennifer rolled off the bed and tiptoed to the garden doorway, hesitating. She'd been told not to go outside.

She snorted. There were no such things as demons.

She slipped into the garden. She could make out buildings all around, some of them with windows glowing from within. And it was so quiet! Most people were indoors for the night. The silence was broken only by bird cries and muffled voices. Somewhere, two cats fought over territory. Something large splashed in the river, sounding closer than it was.

Grandma Jo would have loved it.

"Adventure is where you find it." It was something Grandma Jo always said. In a different country or in your own backyard, it all depended on how you looked at it. This was definitely an adventure. She couldn't explain it, but she felt like she fit in here. She wished Grandma Jo was there to share it.

Had Grandma Jo been worried about her? The dust had sent Jennifer traveling and she was now in Dje-Nefer's body. If Dje-Nefer was in hers, she was probably just as confused as Jennifer was. Jennifer's world might seem a lot stranger to the other girl. At least Jennifer had known something about Dje-Nefer's world. She could speak the language, too. Maybe it was part of being in

86

Dje-Nefer's body. So perhaps Dje-Nefer could talk to Grandma Jo.

Would Grandma Jo have understood what had happened? It would have looked like she'd gone crazy. Jennifer hoped she wouldn't find herself locked in an asylum when she returned. If she returned.

Below on the street, a door creaked open and shut again. She heard Ka-Aper's deep voice rumbling, and Neferhotep's lighter one answering him. She thought she heard him mention her name. Moving as silently as possible, she padded across the cold garden tiles, then bent the reeds apart slightly so she could look down at the street. The two men were right below her.

"I think Dje-Nefer's amulet will protect her," said Neferhotep. "Surely the demons wouldn't be interested in a mere girl."

"Perhaps. I am concerned that she fell asleep in their garden. Has she been acting oddly?"

"A…little."

"A demon may well have bitten her ka. If you like, I can help you put together the herbs and spells of protection. The girl will need to carry it with her for a few days."

"That heart scarab she wears is hollow. She could put it in there."

"Excellent. But we may yet have to perform an exorcism," said Ka-Aper.

"Oh," said Neferhotep. He paused. "Must it come to that?"

"We'll see. Now, you go back in and stay in these wonderfully homey surroundings. I envy you your family."

"They are good people," said Neferhotep. "Are you sure you can't stay? It's so late…"

Ka-Aper laughed, a booming sound that echoed between the buildings. "What? Are you worried that the night demons will attack me? Remember that Ka-Aper is a priest of mighty Amon-Ra. I have my own protections."

"Of course, sir."

"You have stayed up late enough on my account. You go ahead and stay the night. I will see you tomorrow, in the temple."

"Good night, sir, and thank you," said Neferhotep. He reopened the door and slipped into the house.

Jennifer clutched her amulet. So Neferhotep thought she'd been acting strange. She'd have to watch herself more carefully.

Ka-Aper walked down the street. Jennifer was about to pull her head back through the reeds, when she noticed him slowing down. She jerked back as he glanced up. When she peered out again a moment later, he had disappeared.

She squinted, trying to see where he was. There! Just emerging from a house on the corner, a small wrapped bundle in one hand. He slipped it under the leopard skin, then checked the street. Then he strode away, swallowed by the darkness.

"Now what was he doing, sneaking around like that?" Jennifer whispered.

"Dje-Nefer?"

Jennifer turned, stumbling backwards into the reed border. Someone was standing in the doorway.

"Dje-Nefer? What are you doing out here?" It was Mentmose. "Uncle Neferhotep said you weren't suppose to go outside."

"I know," said Jennifer. "I couldn't help it. I heard voices."

"Who?"

"Nefer…I mean, Uncle Neferhotep and…Ka-Aper."

"You shouldn't eavesdrop on people," said Mentmose, frowning. "What were they saying?"

"They were talking about demons," said Jennifer. "You don't believe in demons, do you? Uncle Neferhotep seems to."

"Oh, you know Uncle Neferhotep. He believes in a lot of strange things. He once told me he thought the stars that make up Nut's jewelry might be suns for other lands. And that some day, we could have light without fire. Or buildings that reach to the sky, even higher than the pyramids."

"Well, um," said Jennifer, biting her lip. She didn't think she ought to tell Mentmose that Neferhotep had accurately predicted electricity and skyscrapers!

"He also said he had actually seen Amon-Ra once," said Mentmose, frowning. "I overheard him telling that to Father."

"Really?" asked Jennifer.

Mentmose shrugged. "Anyway, if there are demons, I've never seen one. Now come back inside."

Jennifer gave the bent reeds one more glance. "All right."

"I don't think I like the honorable Ka-Aper," Mentmose said, mostly to himself.

"Me neither," said Jennifer, as they walked back through the garden. "He, um, did a weird thing when I was watching."

"Oh?"

"He got a package from the house down the street," said Jennifer.

"So? Lots of people pick up packages."

"At night?" said Jennifer. "And it was like he didn't want anyone to know what he was doing."

"Well, I'm sure he had a reason. Go back to bed. Teti is still asleep."

"She snores," said Jennifer, as they made their way to the hole where the stairs were. Soft sounds of conversation rose from below.

"One more thing I have to look forward to," Mentmose muttered.

"You should be nicer to her, you know. She's going to be your wife."

"Not for a few years yet, thank Khnum. I still have some freedom. Go." He pushed the curtain aside and went into his half of their room.

Jennifer tiptoed past Tetisheri and tried to lie down, but Miw, the little striped cat, was curled up on her mattress. She eased herself down beside the cat. She chirruped softly, then snuggled in closer when Jennifer pulled the sheet up. As she petted the cat's soft fur, Miw began to purr. Soothed by the sound, Jennifer was soon asleep.

When she woke the next morning, the cat was gone, but Tetisheri was still there, one arm flung over her eyes. She stirred as Jennifer sat up, yawning.

"Good morning," said Jennifer. Tetisheri lowered her arm, blinking against the light.

"Mmmphm," said Tetisheri, covering her face with

her sheet. Jennifer grinned. Apparently, Teti was not a morning person.

"Mentmose, Dje-Nefer, Teti!" Meryt-Re caroled from the stairs. "Breakfast!"

Tetisheri groaned. "So early," she muttered.

Jennifer chuckled and helped Tetisheri to rise. Both girls used the smelly clay pot. When they were ready, they pushed the curtain aside. There had been no awakening sounds from Mentmose.

"Oh, isn't he handsome," said Tetisheri, sighing as she peered down at him.

Jennifer raised one eyebrow at her 'brother.' He was drooling.

"I wonder if I should kiss him awake," said Tetisheri, still watching her betrothed with a dreamy look on her face.

Jennifer thought about the probable consequences. It was tempting, but she didn't hate either of them that much. "No, that's not a good idea," she said, trying not to smile.

She leaned down and shook his shoulder gently, then more firmly.

"Hey, Mentmose, time to get up," she said. She shook him again, as hard as she could.

Mentmose rolled over, falling off his headrest with a thud. Soon he was snoring, his face mashed into the mattress. Jennifer grimaced. Well, if he missed breakfast that wasn't her fault.

Ramose and Meryt-Re were waiting for them in the kitchen, sitting cross-legged on the floor. Bowls of porridge and mugs of tea were set on the striped mat in front of them.

"Where is Neferhotep?" asked Tetisheri.

"He left at dawn, and we have been lolling at our ease since then," said Ramose. "Come and eat. Where is Mentmose?"

"We couldn't wake him," said Jennifer. "He was pretty zon—uh, tired."

Ramose grinned. "I did tell him he should go to bed earlier. But he insisted on staying up to play senet and listen to our talk." He rose and dipped a small bowl into the water jug, then went into the main room. Jennifer could hear him trotting up the stairs. A moment later, there was a loud bellow and several thumps from above.

Tetisheri giggled.

Meryt-Re snorted in amusement as Ramose led a dripping Mentmose into the kitchen.

"Good morning, my bright-eyed son," she said.

Mentmose glared at her, then flopped down on the floor beside Jennifer. "Why didn't you wake me?" he demanded.

"I tried," said Jennifer.

"Really, she did," said Tetisheri, yawning.

Jennifer was tempted to tell Mentmose about Tetisheri's wanting to kiss him awake, but thought she might wait until a better time. The way he was shoveling porridge into his mouth, he might end up spraying it all over the kitchen.

Instead, she picked up her own bowl and started eating. It was the same as yesterday, although this morning there were bits of meat and vegetables in it, probably from last night's leftovers. It was tasty, but she thought she might get tired of having the same thing every day. Visions of waffles and orange juice danced in her head. Maybe she could show Meryt-Re how to make pancakes—Mom had taught her just a few weeks ago. Although it was kind of a lost cause without maple syrup. She hadn't seen any maple trees here. Just lots and lots of date palms.

"Who would like some more?" asked Meryt-Re, lifting the bowl.

"I would," said Ramose, "but I must get to work. Neferhotep said they want more of my amulets. I have completed some, but not all I promised him, so Mentmose and I will have to work hard to finish the rest." He frowned. "I would like to take what I already have to him today, though."

"I have to do the daily shopping," said Meryt-Re, "and today I must see about an allotment of linen for all of us. Perhaps Dje-Nefer and Tetisheri could make the trip to the temple for you. That would give you more time."

"Ah! A wise thought," said Ramose. "Girls, would you mind?"

"Certainly we'll do it, Ramose," said Tetisheri. "I can make my way home from there. Our new house is not far from the temple."

"Good!" said Ramose, rising. He smiled at Meryt-Re.

"Where would I be without you and your good sense?"

Meryt-Re chuckled. "Completely lost, I dare say."

"Too true," said Ramose, kissing her hand.

Tetisheri sighed and smiled. Mentmose rolled his eyes. Ramose rapped him on the head with his knuckles.

"Come, my son, we must go to the workshop."

"Yes, Father," said Mentmose. He gulped the last of his tea, then wiped his face on his wrist and scrambled to follow Ramose.

"This is promising," said Meryt-Re. "I wonder if Ramose will ever be asked to create amulets for the Pharaoh herself."

"My father doesn't approve of the Pharaoh," said Tetisheri, helping herself to more porridge. "He says she ought not to have taken the double crown away from her nephew. He says Thutmose is the rightful king."

Meryt-Re smiled. "Your father is a smart man, but he should be careful what he says. As should you. I have heard of people being sent into the desert for comments like that."

"But—"

"But, nothing, Teti," said Meryt-Re. "Watch your words."

Tetisheri hung her head. "Yes, Meryt-Re."

"Good." She rose and peeked into the water jug. "I think I will get some more water today. I do wish Ramose would remember that we do not have an unlimited supply."

"That's the Pharaoh's fault," Tetisheri muttered. Jennifer glanced at Meryt-Re, but she seemed not to have heard the comment.

"Some day I would like to own a house that has water pipes," said Meryt-Re.

"Like the palace?" asked Tetisheri.

"Yes. Then we wouldn't have to make a trip to the Nile so often. Ah, well. If wishes were horses, beggars would ride."

She turned, just as Ramose strode into the kitchen, carrying a small cloth bag. He opened it to show Meryt-Re.

"Ah," she said, poking through it. She lifted out several pieces and inspected them closely. "These are perfect, as always. Fine work, husband."

"Thank you," said Ramose. He closed up the bag and handed it to Jennifer. "Neferhotep said to take these directly to him."

"Um, all right," said Jennifer.

Tetisheri beamed at Ramose. "Let's go!" She grabbed Jennifer's free hand and pulled her up.

Tetisheri seemed to have regained her voice. She chattered all the way to the temple, mostly about Mentmose and her plans for him. She didn't say anything about Hatshepsut, although she frowned at a man who was selling tiny statues of the Pharaoh, some of them dressed as a man, and some with women's clothing.

All in all, Jennifer was glad of Tetisheri's company. She knew she wouldn't have been able to find the temple without the other girl's help. They wound their way down the streets, already baking in the morning sun, dodging people and animals. They squeezed past a huge black stone statue of a crowned hawk, trying to avoid a lady in her sedan chair.

At one point, they found they couldn't get past a crowd of people who were enjoying the spectacle of two women having a loud argument over a laden donkey, which was placidly munching on some fruit. One of the Pharaoh's white-kilted soldiers was watching, his brawny arms crossed over his chest. He yawned, and didn't seem inclined to interfere until one of the women appealed to him for help. They watched for a moment, then Tetisheri pulled Jennifer away, down a side street shadowed by tall buildings.

When Tetisheri finally pulled her back into the main thoroughfare, Jennifer was completely lost, but Teti seemed to know where she was going.

"Here we are," said Tetisheri, walking boldly towards the temple.

Jennifer probably could have found it on her own, eventually. Even though it was in the middle of a cluster of other buildings, it stood out. It was huge and brightly-painted, decorated over every stone surface with hieroglyphs and larger-than-life depictions of gods and animals. Tetisheri led Jennifer between two massive stone blocks, narrower at their tops than at their bottoms, which stood sentinel on the path to the temple. A bald man, surrounded by clay pots, was touching up the paint on some of the carved characters. Just beyond him, another man was polishing the gold inlay on a stone needle—an obelisk—that pierced the sky in front of the entrance.

Jennifer didn't have time to more than glance at it as Tetisheri hurried inside. They passed out of the bright sunlight into a dark hall where dozens of thick stone pillars grew like trees toward the heavens. They supported gigantic slabs of rock that formed the roof of the temple, so high above her that Jennifer could barely see them.

"What are you doing there?" someone asked. A man dressed in a priest's kilt and leopard skin came striding towards them.

"We're, um," Jennifer stuttered.

"We have a delivery for the honorable Neferhotep," Tetisheri stated in a calm, measured voice. Jennifer stared at her in astonishment.

"A delivery?" The man squinted at them, clearly suspicious.

"Yes, sir. If you would be so pleased as to inform him that we have the amulets he requested," said Tetisheri. "We will wait."

"Amulets, eh? I'll take them for him," said the man.

"I'm sorry, sir," said Tetisheri, with a little curtsey. "But we may not do so."

"Hmph. Come, girl . . ."

"Dje-Nefer? Tetisheri?" Jennifer was relieved to hear Neferhotep's voice. "What are you doing here?"

"They claim they have amulets for you, Nefer," said the man.

"Ah, yes. Thank you, Kai. I will take it from here," said Neferhotep.

The man bowed and wandered away. Neferhotep looked after him, frowning. He turned back to Jennifer and Tetisheri with a bright smile.

"So, Ramose sent you two with my amulets, did he?"

"He was, um, busy," said Jennifer. "Making more amulets."

"Of course. Well, now that you are here, would you like something to drink?" he asked.

"Um," said Jennifer. She wasn't sure she wanted to spend too much time with him. The less time he had to notice her 'strange' behavior, the better. Tetisheri answered too quickly.

"Oh! Yes, please," she said. "We had to walk a long way and we're thirsty."

"Come," said Neferhotep. He led them deeper into the building.

Jennifer couldn't help staring. The pillars were beautiful. Light from grilled windows high above their heads illuminated them, making the colors glow. There was even paint on the undersides of the roof slabs. Jennifer could just make out glimpses of white stars and birds with outstretched wings.

"I never tire of looking at those myself," said Neferhotep. Jennifer jerked her gaze away, but she noticed that Tetisheri was also staring up at the ceiling.

As Neferhotep led them deeper into the temple, Tetisheri told him all about the two women arguing over the donkey, in far more detail than Jennifer had expected her to notice. Neferhotep chuckled at the story. As he brought them to a small room lit by hanging oil lamps, Jennifer realized she was parched. She hoped Neferhotep wasn't going to offer them beer.

A small clay jug, beaded with drops of water, lay on a desk next to a stack of scrolls. Neferhotep gestured for the two girls to sit on a low bed while he moved the scrolls out of the way.

"Now where did I put...? Ah, there they are," he said, moving some clay pots aside to reveal some dusty goblets. He wiped them with a cloth, then poured a clear yellow liquid into them.

Tetisheri eagerly gulped hers down, but Jennifer sniffed at her goblet before sampling. Her eyebrows rose as she recognized it. Grape juice! It was tart, cold and delicious. Both of them held their goblets out for more.

Neferhotep poured more for them and some for himself, then sat on a low-backed chair and shifted the contents of the bag into his hand. His eyes lit up as he saw what it contained.

"Beautiful!" he said, as he picked out a tiny, perfect bird. "Ramose does such fine work. I hope Ka-Aper likes it."

"Are they for him?" asked Jennifer.

"Not necessarily," said Neferhotep, inspecting an ankh the size of his palm, made of green stone. "But he decides what gets wrapped in the linens when mummification is complete. Oh, the deceased gets some say in it, of course, but Ka-Aper is the one who decides what is most appropriate for each stage of the wrapping. Then when he does the Opening of the Mouth ceremony to allow the dead person to partake of speech or food in the afterlife, he can be sure that they have all the protections they will need for the long journey."

The girls sipped their juice and waited politely as he peered at each item. Jennifer gazed around the room. It was filled with small knick-knacks, and shelves full of statues and pots of herbs. Scrolls and blank sheets of papyrus littered the bed beside them. Painted figures of men and women, surrounded by hieroglyphs, covered the walls.

Finally, Neferhotep put all the amulets back in the bag. "Well," he said. "Thank you for bringing these to me."

"You're welcome," said Tetisheri. "Thank you for the juice."

Neferhotep guided them back into the main temple. They were almost at the entrance, when Neferhotep stiffened. He held the girls back.

Jennifer glanced at him curiously. His gaze was fixed

on a young man who was walking towards them, carrying a short golden rod in one hand. He was dressed in a pleated white kilt and a blue and white striped headcloth, with a tiny cobra at his brow. Tetisheri gasped and curtseyed, lowering her eyes, then tugged at Jennifer to do the same.

"Good morning," said the young man. He nodded at Neferhotep.

"Good morning, Prince Thutmose," said Neferhotep, bowing his head.

Jennifer peeked at him from under her hair. So this was Hatshepsut's nephew! He was fit and well-muscled, but not much taller than Jennifer was. Despite that, he seemed to radiate an aura of quiet confidence.

He didn't do more than glance at the two girls before he moved on. Tetisheri stared after him, apparently having trouble breathing.

"That was such an honor!" she said. "Isn't he handsome?"

"His nose is too big," said Jennifer.

"A noble nose," Tetisheri protested. "Like a hawk's. What was he doing here?"

"Making an offering to Amon-Ra, I expect," said Neferhotep. "The Pharaoh often has him perform that important office for her."

"That's all? He should be…" Tetisheri paused, as Jennifer poked her in the side. "Never mind."

"We should get going," said Jennifer.

"Of course," said Neferhotep, eyeing both of them with a slight frown. "Dje-Nefer, would you please tell your mother that I can't join you for dinner this evening? I'm to attend Ka-Aper at the palace."

"Ooh, a palace feast?" asked Tetisheri. "My mother says those are exciting!"

Neferhotep bent down to whisper conspiratorially, "Actually, I find them quite dull."

Tetisheri blushed and giggled. Neferhotep waved them to the entrance, smiling. They emerged out of the cool shadows into the sunlight. The men who had been painting and polishing the obelisk were no longer there.

"I'll walk with you partway, but then I have to get home," said Tetisheri. "Wait till my parents hear that I met Prince Thutmose! They'll be so thrilled."

They hadn't exactly met him, Jennifer thought,

but that didn't seem to matter to Tetisheri. She talked at length about how handsome he was—not as handsome as Mentmose, of course—but thoroughly kingly. Jennifer tried to shush her when they passed a couple of soldiers, but Tetisheri seemed oblivious. One of the soldiers appeared to listen to her chatter for a moment, but let them pass without comment. When Jennifer glanced back at him, he was still watching them, a slight frown on his face.

"Here we are," said Tetisheri. Jennifer looked at their surroundings, but couldn't see anything familiar. "I'll see you later!"

Then Tetisheri was gone, swallowed up by the crowd, leaving Jennifer to find her way home alone. Unfortunately, Jennifer had no idea where she was.

An hour later, Jennifer still hadn't found her way home. She was sure she had come close a few times, but the winding streets had led her into places she'd never seen before. After she encountered the stone hawk for the third time, she realized she was going in circles.

Thirsty, and now with sore feet, she leaned against a wall and watched the people go by. She could ask someone, but who would know? And if they did, wouldn't it seem strange that she didn't know the way to her own home? She peeled herself off the wall and limped away, hot and tired. She thought she could just make out the roof of the temple, beyond one of the stone buildings. Maybe if she returned to it, she could retrace her steps.

Before she reached it, though, she came to a place she recognized. It was the street where the two women had argued about the donkey. It looked like their debate had been resolved. The soldier was still there, telling off a trio of boys carrying handfuls of rocks. He bellowed and they scattered, escaping him, but not before he had landed a couple of smacks on the backs of their heads.

The soldier shook his fist at them, then set off up the street, heading towards Jennifer. In her day, police officers helped lost children, and perhaps the Pharaoh's soldiers did, too. But given Meryt-Re's opinion of them, Jennifer wasn't sure she wanted this one to notice her.

She stepped into the shadowed doorway of one of the tall buildings. The soldier went past her without a glance, and she breathed a sigh of relief. She was about to step out again, but stopped as she saw someone she knew—Ka-Aper. Alone, this time, with no canopy and no attendant boys. He frowned and looked from side to side as he passed her hiding place. Jennifer drew back further into the shadows, squeezing herself flat against the cool stone wall.

Ka-Aper paused, then reached inside his leopard skin and briefly drew out the small wrapped bundle that he had obtained last night while she had been watching. Then he tucked it back inside and patted the skin smooth. With a last glance around, he moved on.

Now what was he up to? Jennifer hesitated, torn between finding her way home and following him. Curiosity won.

She trotted along behind him, keeping his bald head in sight. She tried to make sure several people were always between her and him, so that if he looked around, she could duck behind them for safety. His long strides took him further and further away, and she was forced to jog to avoid losing him. She almost lost him once, but she caught sight of his bald head as he was slipping into a side street just as she passed it. She turned around so she could follow him, bumping into several women behind her. With a muttered apology, she pushed around them so she could double back and catch up with Ka-Aper.

He was gone. No, there he was, just entering a low door set into the side of a shabby, squat building with patches of plaster falling off its sides. Jennifer stopped, wondering where they were. Nowhere near the temple, that was for sure. She couldn't even see its high roof.

The street was deserted. It was quiet, and there were no other exits in the tall walls. She padded down the dusty road, expecting at any moment for him to pop out and see her. There was nowhere she could hide if he did. But he didn't reappear, even when she came to the open doorway.

She stepped over the sill. Inside, it was completely dark. She waited for her eyes to adjust before taking a step forward. There was a faint light coming from the back of the building. Seeds crunched softly under her feet as she stepped between stacks of hundreds of tightly-lidded clay jars, which reached almost to the ceiling. All else was silent. Where was Ka-Aper?

She emerged into an empty area, lit by a flickering oil lamp set on the top of one of the clay jars. It illuminated a dark rectangle set into the floor. Thick dust on the floor carried the imprints of several feet, some bare and some sandaled, all leading to the same place—the hole in the floor. Jennifer peeked into it and saw stairs leading down. Snatches of conversation floated up from it. Her heart thudding, Jennifer crept down the stairs, feeling for each step with her toes.

She was about to set foot on the last one when someone spoke.

"Don't worry, I bribed the guard to stay away for a good long time." It was a man's voice. It was distorted by echoes, but she thought she might have heard it before.

"Our Pharaoh does not have as much control over

her soldiers as she supposes." That voice she recognized. Ka-Aper!

"Neither here nor in the Valley of the Kings," said a third man.

"Speaking of which," said the first man, "when can we expect the next, ah, delivery?"

"Soon," said Ka-Aper. "Parahotep is near death. Seventy days after he dies, and after he is sealed up in his tomb, our men can go to work."

"I've heard that he asked for his tomb to be well-hidden," said the third man.

"Don't they all. His tomb will be a difficult nut to crack," said the first one.

"Yes," said Ka-Aper. His laugh had a nasty edge. "Fortunately, I have a map."

Her hovering foot forgotten, Jennifer covered her mouth as she realized what they were talking about. Parahotep was the man they had discussed at dinner last night. Ka-Aper was a tomb robber!

Jennifer listened closely as the men spoke again.

"Here is the item we spoke about," said Ka-Aper.

"Ah," said the first man. Jennifer heard something

rustle. "Powdered kernels?"

"Untraceable. And imported. The Pharaoh's trading expeditions have borne different fruit from what she planned," said Ka-Aper. They all laughed. "But remember, my name must never be associated with it."

"Of course," said the first man. "It shall be…the will of the gods."

"Hmm, good idea," said Ka-Aper. "Though, if the story of the Pharaoh's birth can be believed, we go against their wishes in this."

The second man laughed. "Oh, come now. Who truly believes that Amon-Ra came to Hatshepsut and revealed that he was her father? And is it not now clear that even the gods themselves are displeased with her?"

"You mean the drought?" asked the first man. "Seven long years, we have suffered. Surely she must know how bad it is."

"Surely," Ka-Aper agreed.

"What we do here is a necessity," said the first man, the one Jennifer thought she knew.

"Absolutely!" said the second man. "Her entire reign is blasphemous. For twenty years, she has paraded herself as

Pharaoh. Why, she even calls herself the female Horus."

"Preposterous!" boomed the first man.

"Habusoneb is wrong," said the second man.

"The High Priest?" asked Ka-Aper. "How can he be wrong?"

"You know it as well as we do," scoffed the first man. "He supports her, but he should not."

"Though it hurts me to say it, Pharaoh Hatshepsut must be chastised for her sin," said Ka-Aper. His voice lowered. "Else her people will feel the wrath of the gods. Indeed, they already do."

Jennifer set her foot down on the last step. As she did so, something sharp jabbed into it. Without looking, she reached down and scooped it up, then leaned closer to the wall to hear better.

"Leave it to us," said the first man.

"Thank you. Remember, I must not know anything about this if I am to play the part properly, so don't tell me when you are going to do it," said Ka-Aper. "When the Pharaoh is dead, I must act as surprised as everyone else."

Jennifer gasped. Dead?

"What was that?" asked one of the men.

"Probably just a mouse," said the other. "With all the grain in this building, they are everywhere. Don't worry about it."

"What, are there no cats? It would seem even Bastet has abandoned our Pharaoh," said the first man, chuckling.

Liquid gurgled into cups.

"And now, some wine to seal the bargain?"

"Please," said Ka-Aper. "In order to disguise where I went last night, I had to endure some truly terrible food and wine. I still haven't gotten the taste of their peasant meal out of my mouth."

"You went to a peasant's house?"

"No. An amulet-maker's. He had some rather mediocre pieces, though a few approached beauty. I'd like to have the scarab he made for his daughter," said Ka-Aper. Jennifer clutched at her amulet. "Ah, that's better. It has a nice bouquet."

"Does it?" asked the first man, slurping.

The second man snorted. "You never could tell bad wine from good."

"Can't smell it, can't taste it," said the first man.

"This is as good as some I've had at the palace," said Ka-Aper.

"It should be," said the second man. "I borrowed it from the Pharaoh herself."

"Ah," said the first man. "To Hatshepsut! Long may she reign." They all laughed.

Jennifer backed slowly up the stairs, moving as quietly as she could.

Ka-Aper wasn't just a tomb robber; he and his friends were planning to kill Hatshepsut, too. She had to warn the Pharaoh, somehow. But it wasn't like she could just waltz up to the palace and expect to be let in. There would probably be soldiers all over the place.

At the top of the stairs, Jennifer let out her breath. She'd made it. She could still hear the men, although she couldn't make out what they were saying. If she could get back to the street, and find the temple, and get home, then all she had to do was figure out a way to let Hatshepsut know what Ka-Aper was up to. She snorted. Easy!

She took a step, and her foot nudged a pebble, which

rolled over the edge of the stairs. She froze as it pinged and rattled all the way to the bottom. There was a sudden silence.

"That was no mouse!" one of the men shouted. "There's someone here!"

Jennifer took off, her bare feet slapping the stone floor. The building's open doorway shone like a beacon in the distance, urging her on. She sprinted towards it, winding her way back through the huge jars, and leaped over the sill, landing in the street with a jarring thud.

Lungs burning, she ran all the way to the end. The main road, where she could lose herself in the crowd, seemed so far away. She reached it and plunged into the mass of people. Risking a quick look behind her, she saw Ka-Aper's bald head just exiting the side street. As the crowd swept her along, he started to look her way. She ducked lower to evade his gaze.

She kept to the middle of the road as people went by her on both sides, and slowed down, a hand clamped over the stitch in her side. She resisted looking over her shoulder. As an extra precaution, in case Ka-Aper was following her, she took a few side trips, going up one unfamiliar street and down another. Once, she thought she heard someone calling her name, but she walked on, eager to get as far from Ka-Aper as possible.

When she thought she had gone far enough, she leaned against a wall, pressing her hand against her side. Her other hand, she was surprised to see, was still curled tight around the item she had picked up on the stairs. She opened it slowly.

Three tiny blue beads the same color as her amulet lay on her palm, strung on a piece of gold wire, which was bent into loops at either end. One of the loops was loose and the other was broken.

Maybe it had come from someone's tomb. Ka-Aper and his thieving friends might have dropped it. Perhaps the warehouse was where they stored their stolen goods. She closed her hand over the fragment. It could be evidence.

She had no pockets in her dress, nor did she have a pouch like Neferhotep's. There was only one place she could keep it. Jennifer flipped open her amulet, then slipped the beads inside it and snapped it shut.

She looked up. Ka-Aper was nowhere to be seen.

But now she was thoroughly lost, and this seemed to be a shabbier part of the city. There were lots of people sitting in the street, some of them watching her. A man gave her a toothless grin when she looked his way. Jennifer pushed away from the wall and walked briskly towards where she thought the temple might be. Two teenagers in ragged kilts watched her pass, their eyes narrowing. Jennifer didn't have anything for them to steal—except her amulet! She quickened her pace.

The sun was definitely higher in the sky than when she and Tetisheri had set out. Meryt-Re might be wondering where she had gotten to. She could maybe ask one of Pharaoh's soldiers for directions, but there didn't seem to be any nearby. Not that she really wanted to approach a soldier—but as she flicked a glance over her shoulder, she saw that the two boys were following her.

She moved a little faster, but another glance showed that they were catching up. She decided to ask someone for help.

There were several people selling broken pots and chunks of stone from blankets set on the cobbles. She hesitated, wondering if any of them would know the house of Ramose the amulet-maker. She was about to head for one of the women, when someone stepped in front of her, blotting out the light.

Jennifer gasped and fell back against the wall.

"Dje-Nefer?" It was a man, silhouetted by the light. He shifted slightly and she saw him clearly then.

"Oh! Um, Uncle Neferhotep. It's you. I thought...," she said, breathing hard. "You scared me."

Neferhotep was breathing hard too. "What are you doing here? I saw you go by and I called out, but you didn't answer."

So that's who it had been. "I'm sorry," she said. "I didn't hear you."

"You're far from the temple," said Neferhotep. "Where were you going?"

"Um...home? But I got lost."

"Lost?" he sounded confused.

"Um, yeah." Jennifer swallowed. Now what? She couldn't tell him where she'd been. He was frowning. "I was walking along, you see, and there was this...accident. A real pile-up. Donkeys everywhere. Someone had crashed into someone else...anyway, I had to detour around it. But then I didn't know where I was. I've been trying to get home, but I ended up here."

She waited to see if Neferhotep was going to buy it. His eyes narrowed as he gazed at her. Finally, he sighed, and said, "I see."

"What about you?" asked Jennifer. "Why are you here?"

"Me?" He scratched his chest. There was a dirty smudge on Neferhotep's kilt, and his eye makeup was starting to smear in the sweat that dripped from his forehead. He looked as though he had been running. "I…had an errand in this part of the city. Well, never mind. The important thing is to get you home."

"You know how to get out of here?" asked Jennifer.

He peered at the buildings around them. "Yes. I mean, I think I do."

"All right."

Neferhotep gestured and Jennifer walked beside him. She glanced at him out of the corner of her eye. He was frowning in concentration, and he gave the impression that he knew where he was going. Maybe this was a place he came often. But why? None of the people who lived here looked like they could afford the kind of funerals that Neferhotep must be used to working on.

Maybe he was involved in Ka-Aper's schemes. How had Ka-Aper gotten that map, anyway? She resolved not to tell him anything about where she'd been and what she'd heard, just in case.

Gradually, they left the poorer section of town. The two boys who had been following her had given up when Neferhotep found her. She flicked another glance at him. Was he really taking her home? If he was part of the tomb robbing gang, he might be taking her to the temple instead. If he knew she'd been listening. Jennifer sighed and rubbed her forehead.

"Something wrong?" asked Neferhotep.

"No, nothing," said Jennifer. "Just a headache."

He fell silent again. A few more minutes' worth of walking brought them to an area she thought she knew, though it was hard to tell. So many of the stone walls looked the same.

"Here we are," said Neferhotep, stopping abruptly.

"We are?" Jennifer looked around. Her gaze lit on the giant bas-relief mural of Thoth, on the school. "Yes. Thank you. I can find my way from here."

"Are you sure?" asked Neferhotep, raising one painted eyebrow.

"Of course!" said Jennifer. She strode boldly down the street, then turned the corner. There was the same house that Ka-Aper had gone into to pick up that bundle last night. The door was tightly shut today. She peeked over her shoulder to see if Neferhotep was watching her, but she couldn't see him. Now...which one was Dje-Nefer's house? They all had flat fronts and wooden doors.

The third house from the corner had a reed fence around the upper floor and a black scarab painted on the outside of the door. Just in case it was the wrong house, Jennifer opened the door cautiously, which swung silently on its well-oiled hinges. Light shone briefly on furniture she recognized. She let out a breath. She had managed to get home without Ka-Aper finding her.

Now all she had to do was explain to Meryt-Re where she had been. She padded across the cool tiles in the main room and looked in the kitchen. It was empty. She listened hard, sure she could hear the faint sound of hammering coming from Ramose's workshop. Perhaps Meryt-Re wasn't back from the market yet. She was safe.

Maybe she ought to pretend she'd been here for a while.

Jennifer wandered around the kitchen, lifting the lids from the various clay pots and jars that lined the shelves, wondering what Dje-Nefer would have been doing if she had found herself alone. More baking? She found large salt crystals and spices hanging from the shelves in colorful little woven baskets, but she didn't know what to do with them.

Maybe she could...stoke the fire, or something. She kneeled on the floor. Using the blackened wooden stick that lay next to the fireplace, she rolled one of the small black coals closer. It was almost perfectly round. She tapped it with the stick and gray ash puffed up.

Maybe it hadn't been dust in her amulet. Maybe it had been ash. She sniffed, and nearly gagged. This stuff didn't smell right.

"There you are," said Meryt-Re. Jennifer jumped. She hadn't heard Meryt-Re come in. "I hope you didn't worry that I was gone so long. There was some sort of procession going on, and I had to go around it. I think it must have been one of the Pharaoh's many foreign friends."

"Were you at the market?" asked Jennifer.

"Yes. Oh, are you feeding the fire? Good. I have some more donkey dung, so you can add that."

Meryt-Re dropped a small bag beside Jennifer, then went to put the water jug away. Jennifer eyed the bag dubiously, then gingerly tipped it over the fire. Several more hard, round balls fell out. Donkey dung? They'd been cooking over donkey dung? Suddenly, she felt a bit nauseated.

"I swear the Nile is even lower today," said Meryt-Re, shaking her head. "I had to wade out in it to get our water. Lucky for me, there were soldiers posted on the shore to keep an eye out for crocodiles and water oxen." She took the bag from Jennifer. "I saw Neferhotep outside."

"Y-you did?" asked Jennifer.

"He asked if you'd made it home all right," said Meryt-Re. "I said I was sure you had. He was on his way back to the temple."

"Oh," said Jennifer.

Meryt-Re was about to speak again, when they both heard a knocking on the front door. "That must be him again. I wonder what he wants? Would you go answer it, please?"

Jennifer crossed the main room and flung open the door.

"Yes?" she said.

Ka-Aper towered in the doorway.

Jennifer's mouth went dry. "C-can I help you?" she croaked.

The priest smiled down at her. "Is your father within?"

"He's in the workshop," said Jennifer, clutching the side of the door. "I think."

"Good. I wish to speak with him." He waited patiently, still smiling. After a moment, he said, "May I come in?"

"Uh, sure," said Jennifer. She opened the door wider, and he strode in.

"After you," he said, gesturing that she should go first.

"Oh. Right," said Jennifer. She paused, realizing that she didn't exactly know where Ramose's workshop was. But there was a curtained doorway at the back of the room, near the stairs. Muffled hammering sounds came from behind it.

Jennifer led Ka-Aper to the curtain, feeling all the while like he was following too close. She pushed the curtain aside and went in, Ka-Aper right behind her.

Ramose was there, one hand on a tiny amulet, the other just raising a bronze tool. He looked up as Jennifer entered, then shot to his feet. His face broke into a cautious smile.

"Sir!" he said. "You honor us once more. What may I do for you?"

"My good Ramose," said Ka-Aper, pushing past Jennifer, "I must speak with you on a matter of importance."

His voice lowered. Mentmose, who had been industriously tapping away at something on his bench, put his hammer down. Jennifer strained to hear what Ka-Aper was saying to Ramose.

"Dje-Nefer!" said Meryt-Re, from behind her, making her jump. Mentmose jerked, and quickly picked up his hammer again. Meryt-Re raised one eyebrow at Jennifer and pointed towards the kitchen.

"I need you to clean out the ashes, please," she said.

Jennifer scurried across the main room and kneeled in front of the fireplace. Spying a little clay scoop, she picked it up and shoved it into a pile of warm ashes. A plain, blackened pot was half-hidden behind the fireplace. It was empty, but there was a little ash residue in the bottom. She dumped the ash in there, coughing a little as the fine dust puffed up. Jennifer dug into the fire with her scoop and glanced at Meryt-Re, who was intent on wiping some dishes that she neatly packed away into a wicker basket. She wasn't watching Jennifer.

"What...do you suppose he wants?" she asked.

"Ka-Aper? None of your business, young lady," said Meryt-Re. "Although I wouldn't be surprised if he was asking for more of your father's work." She frowned, and her voice lowered to a murmur. "I hope he plans to give us something for it. I know Neferhotep will give us another papyrus for the ones you gave him as soon as he can. But he says some priests think they ought to be given items like that for free."

Ka-Aper didn't even bother asking. He just stole them. Jennifer thought about telling Meryt-Re, but she doubted she'd be believed. She glanced at the door to the kitchen. She was sure he had seen her running away from the warehouse, and even now he might be telling her father how she had spied on him and his friends. She bet he could get the soldiers to arrest her, somehow, and throw her in jail, and she might never get out again.

Now might be a good time to try to get back to her own time. Dust from the amulet had brought her here; she was sure of that. The dust would probably take her back too. If it was the right kind of dust.

It hadn't been ashes, she was sure. Maybe it was fine sand, like the stuff in the streets. She rose.

"Where are you going?" asked Meryt-Re.

"Uh," said Jennifer. "Outside?"

"Whatever for?" asked Meryt-Re. "Come back and finish building the fire for me."

Jennifer sighed, turning back to the hearth. Ash, still drifting in the air, made her cough. She walked over to the full water jug and dipped an empty cup into it. She was about to set it to her dry lips when Meryt-Re gasped.

"What are you doing?" she cried.

"I'm thirsty," said Jennifer.

"And you were going to drink fresh Nile water?" said Meryt-Re, frowning. "What's gotten into you?"

"Uh…"

"Don't you remember Uncle Neferhotep telling us not to drink it while the Nile is so low? He says it would make us ill, and that we should only use it for washing, or boil it before using it," said Meryt-Re, her hands on her hips. "If you're so thirsty, I'll get you some beer."

"Uh, no, that's all right," said Jennifer.

"Are you thirsty or not? Make up your mind. Well. Have you finished with the fireplace?" asked Meryt-Re.

"What? Oh. Yeah, I guess I have," said Jennifer.

"Take the ashes upstairs and spread them on the garden then," said Meryt-Re.

"Oh. Sure."

Meryt-Re gave her an odd look. Jennifer hefted the blackened pot and carried it up to the second floor. As she scattered the ashes around the garden, she could hear Meryt-Re puttering in the kitchen. The front door opened and closed. She couldn't resist peeking over the edge of the house again.

This time, Ka-Aper stood squarely in the street, looking directly up at her. He gave her a cheery little salute, then strode out of sight.

She shivered. Ka-Aper scared her. She had to find a way to get out of here.

When she returned to the kitchen, Ramose, Meryt-Re and Mentmose were all there waiting for her. Ramose was smiling, but Meryt-Re seemed concerned. Mentmose just looked baffled. Jennifer swallowed. Here it came.

"There you are," said Ramose, as Jennifer entered. "We were waiting for you. As I was telling your mother, I have good news."

"G-good news?" asked Jennifer, startled.

"What is it, Father?" asked Mentmose.

Ramose grinned. "We have been invited to dinner at the palace!"

"Ra!" exclaimed Mentmose. "The palace! Will the Pharaoh be there?"

"I expect so," said Ramose, chuckling. "It's where she lives. She is holding a feast tonight to honor the arrival of the emissary from Punt. Ka-Aper wanted to do us a favor, to get us introduced at the Pharaoh's court."

"But Ramose, the expense," said Meryt-Re. "We will need new clothes and jewelry. And wigs and scent, and…"

"For which I will give you some of my carvings, and you can work your bartering magic upon the vendors," said Ramose.

"These items will be very expensive, Ramose. For a dinner at the palace, we must have extraordinary outfits," said Meryt-Re. "Else the other guests will look down on us."

"Get whatever you need," said Ramose.

Meryt-Re sighed. "I don't suppose the great Ka-Aper gave you a temple papyrus," she said.

"Well, no," said Ramose. "But I could hardly ask."

"I guess not. I wish…"

"Mother! This is a wonderful opportunity," said Mentmose. "The palace! If the Pharaoh takes note of father and his artistry…"

"I could possibly get a royal commission," said Ramose. "The temple is good to me, but if I had royal attention? Think of it."

"If you had royal favor," said Meryt-Re, putting a hand to her lips, "we might be able to afford a villa in the country."

"Yes! We could move. Have servants! A chariot and horses. Indoor plumbing. All manner of lovely things for you to enjoy," said Ramose.

"Oh, Ramose," said Meryt-Re. "What a wonderful thought. So. We will need two full outfits…"

"Four."

"Four?"

"Yes, the children are invited, too," said Ramose.

Mentmose whooped. "The palace! I get to go to the palace!"

"But Ramose…I don't know how we can possibly afford that," said Meryt-Re. "I think the children will have to stay home."

"Oh, mother, please!" said Mentmose. "I'll do anything. Only let me come."

Meryt-Re pursed her lips.

"I'm afraid we have no choice," said Ramose. "Ka-Aper specifically told me to bring them just before he left."

"What? But why?" asked Meryt-Re.

Jennifer wondered that, too.

"I don't know," said Ramose. "He didn't say."

"Oh, very well," said Meryt-Re. Mentmose whooped again. "But Ramose, you will have to be satisfied with what I can find. I will need your best work."

"You shall have it," he promised. He left the kitchen, returning only a few moments later with a handful of carvings. "I've been saving these."

"Careful," said Meryt-Re, taking them from him, one by one. "Oh, my. Ptah does guide your hand, Ramose. These are beautiful."

She held a small blue hippopotamus up to the light. To Jennifer's eyes, the little animal seemed almost alive.

"That is one of my favorites," said Ramose, smiling at the hippo.

"Sacred to Tawaret," said Meryt-Re, narrowing her eyes. "I'll see if I can trade this to someone who is expecting a child."

"That's a good idea," said Ramose. "Mentmose, we have more work to do."

"Come, Dje-Nefer," said Meryt-Re. "We should

start now."

"I leave it in your capable hands," said Ramose.

Meryt-Re rolled her eyes as he and Mentmose left. "Men," she murmured. "They think things just happen."

Jennifer couldn't help giggling. Meryt-Re sounded just like her own mother.

"Let us be off, then," said Meryt-Re. "If it does further your father's career, it will have been worth it."

Jennifer nodded. They were going to the palace!

Maybe she could figure out a way to get to the Pharaoh before Ka-Aper did.

The market was just as noisy and crowded as it had been the day before. Meryt-Re had set out from the house at a brisk pace, Jennifer trotting along behind her. As soon as they reached the rabbit warren of stalls and booths, Meryt-Re slowed to a saunter. Unlike yesterday's efficient trip, today she acted like she had all the time in the world.

First, she traded a few of her good barley cakes for some pieces of dried fruit. Jennifer frowned as they stopped at yet another food-seller's stall. Meryt-Re didn't seem in the least bit interested in the booths that displayed outfits or jewelry.

"Aren't we…?" she started to ask.

"Hush," said Meryt-Re, with a little smile. "Patience."

More fruit, some vegetables and a small chunk of that delicious white cheese steadily replaced the cakes in Meryt-Re's basket. While Jennifer waited outside, Meryt-Re slipped into a covered stall that smelled of pungent herbs and perfumes.

Right next to a vegetable vendor was a man selling

musical instruments. He handed something that looked like an oversized metal wishbone to a white-clad woman. She shook it, jingling several bells that were strung across thin wires between its two metal arms.

Meryt-Re returned from the perfumery with a small, tightly-stoppered bottle which she carefully positioned in the bottom of the basket.

"I had to trade two of your father's amulets for that," she confided to Jennifer. "The perfume merchant said he would present them to his mother, since she is preparing her tomb for her burial. But I think he might keep them."

A little more wandering took them deeper into the market. But before they could get very far, a crowd formed, standing to watch something that was accompanied by the sounds of harps and bells and brass trumpeting.

"Oh!" said Meryt-Re. "A funeral procession. It sounds like an expensive one. Let's watch."

She pulled Jennifer through the crowd, easing them closer to the front of the hundreds of people, where they could see better.

It was a glittering sight. First came an old woman and a younger one, both of them weeping loudly and throwing ash in their hair. They were followed by a sarcophagus on a wooden sledge, pulled by four huge horned oxen, straining at their harness. The sarcophagus wasn't solid gold, like Tutankhamen's coffin, but it had gold inlay, and the rest of it was painted with vivid reds, blues and oranges. Several people lent a hand to the ropes, keeping the oxen in line. Like the first two women, they were crying and waving their arms.

Behind them were eight women in long blue dresses, their hair wild and lines of black tears painted on their cheeks. They bawled and wailed, making more noise than all the others combined.

"My goodness!" said Meryt-Re. "Eight professional mourners! What an expense. I wanted to be a mourner when I was younger. Then I married your father, and I soon had other things on my mind." She smiled down at Jennifer.

Following the mourners came other people, even children, all walking at a dignified pace; then several others, carrying clothing, food, racks of tiny statues, golden

140

chests, and even pieces of furniture. Two of them pulled a sledge carrying four squat jars with stoppers shaped like heads of men and animals, which Jennifer realized must be the mummy's canopic jars. Last to come were the musicians, strumming hand-held harps, blowing horns, and shaking instruments like the one Jennifer had seen being sold earlier. Long-eared dogs yapped and ran after them. Finally, the procession was gone and all was quiet. The hum of the market started up again.

Meryt-Re bowed her head. "May Ma'at guard his ka," she said.

"Did you know him?" asked Jennifer.

"No," said Meryt-Re. "By the look of his procession, he was probably some noble from the court. I wonder if Ka-Aper will perform the Opening of the Mouth ceremony for him. I hope it goes well, or this fellow will not be able to partake of the food that gets buried with him."

"I hope the tomb robbers don't get to him," said Jennifer.

"Dje-Nefer, don't be so gloomy," said someone from behind Jennifer.

She turned. Tetisheri beamed at her.

"What are you doing here?" Jennifer blurted.

"Same as you," said Tetisheri. "Aren't funerals beautiful?"

"Beautiful? But he's dead," said Jennifer.

Tetisheri looked puzzled. "Of course, but his mummy will soon be reborn to a new life and will be honored at the gods' side."

"Hm," said Jennifer. The mummy in the museum hadn't looked reborn at all. It was still pretty dead.

"Were you shopping?" asked Tetisheri.

"Yes, for clothing," said Jennifer.

"Clothing? Why?" said Tetisheri. "Your mother usually makes your clothes, doesn't she? Are you going somewhere special? I know! You're having dinner with Ka-Aper again, aren't you?"

Meryt-Re put her hand on Jennifer's shoulder and gave it a squeeze. When she spoke, it was barely above a murmur. "Actually, we are going to the feast at the palace tonight."

"Oh! So am I!" Tetisheri squealed.

"Your family has been invited as well?" asked Meryt-Re.

"Of course!" said Tetisheri. "My father is the second assistant official to the Curator of Monuments."

"I had forgotten his new position. Of course he would be going."

"This time, I get to go, too. Mother just told me. Do you think Mentmose would like to escort me?" Tetisheri asked, blushing slightly.

Jennifer stifled a snort.

"Perhaps we could all go together," Meryt-Re suggested.

"What a good idea!" said Tetisheri, beaming. "I'll go tell my parents." She dashed away, and melted into the crowd.

"What does a Curator of Monuments do?" asked Jennifer, hoping that Dje-Nefer wouldn't know that.

"I am not entirely sure," said Meryt-Re, smiling, "but you can be certain that it is a very, very important job. At least, so Tetisheri's mother told me." She sighed. "She also hinted that Tetisheri's betrothal to Mentmose may no longer be…appropriate."

"That would make Mentmose happy," said Jennifer.

Meryt-Re's smile tilted. "I know he is not pleased

with our choice of a wife for him. Satyah and I were close friends when we were younger and pledged to match our children together. When you were all small and her husband not so exalted, it seemed no hardship for her. But now...well. Anyway, Mentmose should be grateful. Tetisheri is devoted to him, despite her mother's recent objections. He could do much worse."

"She talks too much, but she's nice," said Jennifer.

Meryt-Re laughed. "A fair assessment. Now let us be about our own business."

"Will Tetisheri be shopping for new clothes, too?" asked Jennifer.

"Likely they already have outfits being custom-made for them. Satyah hired a seamstress as soon as Hekhanakhte was appointed to his new office." Meryt-Re started walking again, steering Jennifer away from the market and down a narrow side street.

"I thought we were going to buy clothes," said Jennifer.

"We are," said Meryt-Re. "As you so aptly put it, Tetisheri talks too much. She has probably told several people by now that we are all going to the feast."

"So?"

"So, clothing vendors in our market may hear it and would then know that we are in need of their wares. The price would go up because of that. It is always better to pretend that you are not interested in what they have to sell. We will go to a different market where they do not know us so well. And hope that no one there knows Tetisheri!"

"Will they have what we need?" asked Jennifer, trying to keep up with Meryt-Re's quickening pace.

"That is a chance we will have to take," said Meryt-Re.

They emerged from the shaded, twisting road into a sunlit open area. Jennifer nearly bumped into Meryt-Re, as she slowed her rapid walk to a leisurely saunter. Jennifer strolled along beside her, trying to match her calm survey of the vendors.

Like the other market, this one was filled with a disordered jumble of booths, a path of beaten earth winding between them. They passed more sellers of pottery, brass items and vegetables, and even someone sitting under an umbrella, cross-legged on a mat. He was writing a letter that was being dictated to him by a well-dressed nobleman.

"A scribe," murmured Meryt-Re. "This market must be frequented by some of the upper classes. We shall see what we can find."

The scribe dipped his reed pen into an inkwell on a leather strap strapped across his bare chest, nodded to his customer, and continued writing. Jennifer tried to peek at the letter, but Meryt-Re wouldn't let her.

"What are you doing?" she asked.

"I just wanted to see the hieroglyphs," said Jennifer.

Meryt-Re shook her head. "Why? Neither you nor I would be able to read them. That's a man's job. I don't know what's gotten into you. First asking about school, now this. Bad enough that your father lets you play at painting our walls."

"Paint?" said Jennifer. Her mouth opened in surprise. So that's who the artist was. Dje-Nefer! "But they're good!"

"Don't go getting ideas above yourself, Dje-Nefer." Meryt-Re frowned. "Your painting is just for fun. You'll have to give it up soon."

"Why?"

"Because you'll be too busy with women's work. It is work, you know, no matter that you might not yet understand that." Meryt-Re gave Jennifer a speculative look as they hurried on. "Perhaps we have already indulged your hobby for too long."

Jennifer gulped. She hadn't meant to get Dje-Nefer in trouble.

"Here we are," said Meryt-Re, with a swift glance at a nearby booth, where several men's kilts hung from poles. The seller also had piles of linen on his tables.

But instead of looking directly at the booth, Meryt-Re fingered a pile of dark woolen blankets stacked neatly under a nearby awning. The man selling them oozed up beside her and chattered away about how fine they were, and how useful they would be after the annual Nile flood, when it got so much colder. Jennifer could tell that Meryt-Re was only half-listening to him.

"Weren't we looking for...," Jennifer began.

"Sh," said Meryt-Re. Jennifer looked at her, confused. But Meryt-Re gave her a tiny nod, and the ghost of a wink. She left the blanket seller and sauntered past the one with the men's outfits. The man in the booth turned their way as they passed.

"Something for your husband, mistress?" he asked, showing a lot of teeth.

Meryt-Re pretended not to be interested, but eventually she let him talk her into looking at two. Bargaining for the kilts went slowly, with the man insisting that Meryt-Re was the most beautiful woman he had ever seen—barring the Pharaoh herself, of course—and that times were so hard, he needed her to be as generous as she was lovely. In the end, Meryt-Re reluctantly handed over an onyx sheep, a malachite horse, and two turquoise elephants for two fine linen shirts, two sheer linen tunics, and a pair of beaded pectorals.

Meryt-Re sighed when they left. "As I suspected, wares in this market are somewhat more expensive than where I usually shop. The quality is very good. Let us see if we can find some outfits for ourselves now. Or at least for me. We may not have enough for a new dress for you."

"That's all right," said Jennifer.

A little further away, they found a booth offering women's clothing, next to a cheese seller's booth. Stretched across the fabric of a large covered booth were several outfits, sparkling in the sun. Jennifer sucked in a breath at their opulence. The golden belt and collar on a long white dress shimmered in the sun as a breeze rippled the awning.

"Lovely, aren't they?" Meryt-Re murmured. "Shall we look at the cheese?" she said in a louder voice.

Jennifer obediently inspected cheeses with Meryt-Re, giving the clothing booth an occasional glance. In the shade of the canopy, a gray-haired woman was bargaining with a customer, who finally agreed to a price. With a handshake and a nod, the woman accepted something in exchange, passed across the table in front of her. A teenage boy stood close beside her. He wrapped the merchandise in a piece of fabric and handed it to the customer.

"Let's go," said Meryt-Re. She shook her head at the man selling the cheeses. He was still trying to get her to buy one even as she walked away.

As they approached the clothing booth, the old woman came out of the shadow of her awning and smiled at them. Jennifer gasped.

"Grandma Jo?"

"Pardon?" said the old woman.

"Grandma Jo!"

The old woman flicked a puzzled glance at Meryt-Re, then stared at Jennifer. "Do I know you, dear?"

"Are...aren't you...," Jennifer began.

Meryt-Re gazed at Jennifer with a baffled expression. "Dje-Nefer? Are you all right?"

Jennifer stared. "I, uh," she stammered, clutching her scarab amulet. "I thought...never mind."

The resemblance was amazing, even though the woman's braided gray hair was longer than Grandma Jo's ever had been. Her eyes were outlined with a thick line of dark green kohl, and her skin was darker than either Meryt-Re's or Jennifer's. Could it be Grandma Jo? But surely, she would have said something, if she was.

The old woman shrugged, then turned to Meryt-Re, who was eyeing Jennifer with a most peculiar expression. "May I help you, dear?"

"No, no, thank you. We were just looking."

"For anything in particular?"

"My daughter was just admiring one of your outfits," said Meryt-Re.

"Which one?" asked the woman, all business.

"The white one, with the beaded collar," said Meryt-Re. "But we really can't take the time to look at it. We have so much to do."

"Wait, I have one just like it in the back. Ti, go get it, please."

The boy trotted behind her, into a closed-off area in the rear of the tent.

"My grandson," said the old woman.

"A fine boy," said Meryt-Re. The woman beamed at her.

Ti soon returned, carefully carrying a folded dress and a small wooden box. The woman took the dress from him and shook it out in front of Meryt-Re. Ti lifted a layered collar of green beads from the box and held it up in front of Jennifer, grinning at her.

"It's nice," said Meryt-Re. "What are you asking?"

"Two deben of gold," said the woman.

"Mm. Well, perhaps some other time," said Meryt-Re, turning away. "My clothing chest is full enough."

The old woman raised one eyebrow. "Surely a lady such as yourself could make room for one more? You deserve finery, my dear."

"Don't we all," said Meryt-Re, laughing. "Thank you, but we really must be on our way."

The woman leaned closer to Meryt-Re and laid the dress on the table. "But can you not see yourself in this? The beads of the pectoral are made of the very best malachite, perfect for your complexion."

"Well…," said Meryt-Re, bending to examine the dress more thoroughly. "It is lovely. But see? There is a flaw in the linen."

Jennifer squinted at the spot where Meryt-Re was pointing. She couldn't make out more than a tiny bump on the surface.

"The malachite in the collar is pretty, but I know where I can get better," Meryt-Re continued.

"I assure you, you will not find clothing superior to mine," said the old woman.

"My grandmother Mutemwija makes the best," said Ti, scowling.

"Hush, boy," said Mutemwija. "You are right

about the flaw, however. Perhaps we could come to an agreement."

"I'm not carrying any gold with me today," Meryt-Re said loftily. "I have this."

She rummaged in her basket and pulled out one of Ramose's carvings, a translucent, white sitting cat. Its eyes were made of pale green chips.

Ti's eyebrows flew up and then back down again so swiftly that Jennifer wasn't sure if she had imagined it. Mutemwija's face was expressionless as she took the cat from Meryt-Re and inspected, much as Meryt-Re had done with the dress, looking for flaws. Jennifer stroked her scarab amulet and doubted she would find any.

"Quartz, is it?" asked Mutemwija, glancing at Meryt-Re. "This might be enough for the gown, but not the necklace also."

"Quartz is difficult to carve," said Meryt-Re, with a toss of her black hair. "My husband Ramose is one of the finest stone artists in all of Kemet. Ptah guides his hand—as surely as he does yours. He is the exclusive supplier of amulets to a high priest of Amon-Ra."

Mutemwija turned the cat over to look at the base. "I

suppose this is meant for a tomb, then? It is very fine, but as I say, not quite enough. Now, if you had something to go with it…"

Meryt-Re retrieved another carving, twin to the first, but made of turquoise, and with the cat's tail curving in the opposite direction. This cat's eyes were black.

"Ahhhh," said Mutemwija. "A matched set. Very well. The cats for the dress and the pectoral, and we have a bargain."

"I accept," said Meryt-Re, offering her hand for the woman to shake. "Now we really must be moving on."

Ti wrapped up the dress and necklace and handed it to Meryt-Re, who slipped it into her basket.

"May one ask if the lady will be wearing my creation somewhere special? I must say, it is one of my favorites," said Mutemwija.

Meryt-Re leaned conspiratorially closer. "The palace!" she said. "My family and I have been invited to dine there this evening. Have we not, Dje-Nefer?"

"Ra! That's an honor," said Mutemwija, smiling at Jennifer. "Dje-Nefer, is it?" She slurred the name, making it sound more like Jennifer's. "May I know your name?"

"It's Meryt-Re," said Meryt-Re. She glanced at the sun. "But we really must…"

"Wait," said Mutemwija. She whispered something to Ti, who then trotted to the back. When he returned, he was carrying a small bundle under his arm. Mutemwija took it from him, then handed it to Meryt-Re.

With a puzzled frown, Meryt-Re shook it out. It was a dress like hers, but in a smaller size.

"Will that fit your daughter?" asked Mutemwija.

"Well, yes, but I can't…"

Mutemwija held up her hand, palm outward. "A gift. For your little girl. She reminds me of my daughter's daughter."

"A gift?" said Meryt-Re.

"A gift?" Ti squawked, looking appalled.

Mutemwija patted him on the shoulder. "Yes. And if you should happen to mention my name at the palace tonight…"

Ti's expression cleared.

"Of course," said Meryt-Re. "I will tell as many people as possible where I got this lovely outfit."

"I would be grateful," said Mutemwija. "My grandson

and I have only recently arrived from the south."

"So you do not yet have a large client base," said Meryt-Re. "I see. I will do what I can. The quality of your work speaks for itself."

"Thank you," said Mutemwija.

Meryt-Re inclined her head and walked away. Jennifer followed, sneaking a glance over her shoulder.

Mutemwija was staring after them. She raised her hand in farewell, then turned to talk with another customer.

"I am very pleased," Meryt-Re confessed to Jennifer. "I can't believe we got my new outfit for only two of Ramose's carvings."

"Is that good?" asked Jennifer.

"Oh, yes, very good. I was expecting to have to use more. The quality of this outfit—of both of them—is exceptional. I would have recommended her to others even if she had not asked me to. She will have to learn to price her wares accordingly if she is hoping to do well in this market."

"She…was very nice," said Jennifer, looking over her shoulder once again. Mutemwija's booth was no longer visible. "Maybe she liked you."

"I think it more likely that she liked you," said Meryt-Re. "You heard her say you reminded her of her granddaughter."

Mutemwija had certainly reminded her of Grandma Jo, so the feeling was mutual.

"It's so sad that your grandmother is no longer alive," said Meryt-Re.

"What?" squeaked Jennifer.

"Pardon?" Meryt-Re frowned at her.

"But she...uh, sorry. I just didn't hear you clearly," said Jennifer.

Meryt-Re gave her an odd look, but didn't say anything else. They rounded a corner of the market, to see a woman walking towards them with a black wig carefully balanced on a wooden stand.

"That's the next thing we need to purchase," said Meryt-Re.

To Jennifer's newly-educated eyes, bartering for the wigs seemed to go well enough, although Meryt-Re didn't seem as happy about the trade as she had been for the other items. She exchanged an orange-red ankh, two miniature headrests, an Eye of Horus carved from the same dark blue stone as her scarab, and the hippo, since the man's wife was expecting their third child.

"Well, they are real hair," said Meryt-Re, as they walked away. "It was worth it."

"Are we done?" asked Jennifer. She was sure that the sunlight beating down on her shoulders was giving her a sunburn..

"Almost," said Meryt-Re. "We just need to buy sandals. The clothing vendor told me that old Khufu, across the market, makes the best."

"Was he telling the truth?" asked Jennifer, wriggling her sore bare feet.

"Oh, Khufu is probably his cousin or something, but I have no doubt he makes good sandals, or he would not have recommended him. Angry customers would only bring him misfortune."

"I wonder if he's going to tell Khufu we're coming," said Jennifer, thinking about the secrecy that Meryt-Re had wanted to keep, so that she could get better bargains.

"Possibly," said Meryt-Re. "Let us see if we can outfly

the news. However, I had a reason for asking about sandals. Now he knows that Ramose the amulet-maker is moving up in the world. He will tell others."

Old Khufu did indeed make superior footwear, and Meryt-Re was able to trade two pieces from her hoard for four pairs of leather-soled sandals. She had Jennifer carry them.

Since they had gone to a different market, it took longer to get home. By the time they returned to the house, Jennifer was ready for a nap.

She sagged against the wall of the main room, as Meryt-Re placed her basket carefully on the floor. Ramose appeared from his workshop, followed by a very dirty Mentmose.

"Well?" asked Ramose. "How did it go?"

"Not as well as I could have wished, but well enough," said Meryt-Re. She dug under the clothing and handed the nearly empty bag of carvings to him.

"Oh, good," said Ramose. "I was hoping to present some pieces to the Pharaoh. I thought they would all be gone."

"I'm a better bargainer than that," said Meryt-Re.

Jennifer laid the sandals on the floor and helped her unpack the baskets.

"I know, I know. I was just teasing. And what did you…?" He let out a low whistle as Meryt-Re held up the clothing, the wigs and the jewelry. "Ptah! You bought all this, and still had some carvings left over?"

"Yes, Ramose."

"I had no idea you were as good a bargainer as this," he said. "Perhaps I should send you when next I want to obtain stones from the miners. Dear one, I am most impressed."

"I admit we got some of the items for a better trade than I expected," said Meryt-Re. "But the other trades were good, too. I could not have done so well if it were not for the quality of your work. It is your loving touch upon the stones that impresses them, Ramose."

Ramose grinned and picked up the little bottle that Meryt-Re had set on the floor and wiggled the stopper out.

"Careful," said Meryt-Re.

Ramose sniffed at it. "Lotus oil?"

"Yes," said Meryt-Re. "Although, I would have liked

something more exotic, like spikenard or myrrh."

"I'm told myrrh is the Pharaoh's favorite scent," said Ramose. "Neferhotep said she had several myrrh trees brought from Punt. They have been planted in front of her mortuary temple."

"We are not so fortunate. Lotus will have to do for us," said Meryt-Re.

"Is this for me?" asked Mentmose, as he picked up one of the men's outfits. His eyes grew round as he looked at it.

"Yes, my son," said Ramose. "Women will be talking of your beauty for years to come."

"Perhaps even the Pharaoh herself will notice you," added Ramose, grinning at Mentmose's blush, visible even on his dark skin.

"Only if you wash." Meryt-Re snatched the outfit out of Mentmose's filthy fingers and examined it for smudges. "Did you know you have stone powder on your nose?"

"I bet Tetisheri will like it," said Jennifer, looking at him out of the corner of her eye.

Mentmose glared at her, then smiled good-naturedly.

"Dinner at the palace! My friends will be so envious. I wonder if we will be seated anywhere near Her Majesty?"

"Probably not," said Meryt-Re. "Now, we must dash to the river to wash."

The four of them paraded down the streets to the banks of the Nile, where several soldiers stood on guard, looking out across the water. After a brief discussion, Meryt-Re and Ramose chose the driest path they could find, trying to avoid the sticky black mud. The path passed near a thick patch of spiky plants.

"It's too dangerous," said Meryt-Re. "There may be crocodiles."

"It's either that or mud to the knees," argued Ramose. "Besides, the soldiers would have warned us if they'd seen any."

Meryt-Re shook her head. "We still must be very careful," she said, as she waded into the water and stripped off her dress, letting it float in the current. Ramose and Mentmose followed.

Jennifer glanced nervously up and down the river. There were a few boys in the distance, playing with sticks and stones, but no one seemed to be watching her. She made her way out to where the others were splashing and ducking and started to pull off her dress. A movement in the rushes caught her gaze and she stood still.

Two piggy black eyes stared back at her, framed in a fleshy pink and brown face, just rising above the surface of the water. Small ears twitched.

"Hey, look," she said. "A hippo!"

"What?" said Mentmose, as he emerged from the water, wrapping his wet kilt around his hips.

"A hippopotamus," said Jennifer, pointing. "In there."

Mentmose looked, then froze. "Pehemau," he whispered. Jennifer's ears translated it as "water ox."

Ramose and Meryt-Re splashed nearer. Mentmose silently held up a hand, warding them off. He shooed them away from the rushes. The hippo rose out of the water, water streaming from its sides.

As Meryt-Re and Ramose angled away from the plants, Mentmose grabbed Jennifer's shoulder and backed slowly away from the huge animal.

The hippo eyed them, then settled back into the river, water squirting up from beneath its powerful body.

"Ra," said Mentmose, as they made it to the riverbank.

"That was close."

"It was just a hippo," said Jennifer.

"What do you mean?" Mentmose shook his head. "Little sisters are so stupid. If that water ox had been more interested in defending its territory, we'd all be dead. Now, come on."

Ramose and Meryt-Re joined them, their wet clothes clinging to their bodies.

"Did you see a crocodile?" asked Ramose.

"No," said Mentmose. "A water ox."

Meryt-Re's face paled. "Thank the gods you were not hurt. And that you warned us." She looked at Jennifer. "Did you not even get clean?"

"Uh, no," said Jennifer. She glanced at Mentmose. He was frowning at her.

"It is too late now. You will have to wash off at home."

They informed the guards of the presence of the hippopotamus and headed back to the house.

Meryt-Re let Jennifer wipe herself down with a damp cloth while Ramose and Mentmose went to don their new finery. When they were all dressed, they assembled in the main room.

"Well, now," said Meryt-Re. "Don't we look like we belong in noble society."

"We will shine, my dear," said Ramose.

Mentmose stroked the sheer linen of his tunic. The fine material of the men's long, short-sleeved tunics was nearly transparent and showed off their well-muscled chests. Under the tunics, the spotless white pleated kilts reached nearly to their knees. A piece of the same fabric was wrapped neatly around their hips, like a wide belt. Jennifer had thought they would look funny in their new outfits, but they looked…right.

The short-sleeved white dress that Jennifer now wore fit her perfectly, as did the translucent outer dress, which was belted tight to her waist with a piece of fabric. The outer dress was really just a rectangle of linen with a circle cut out for her head, but Meryt-Re had arranged it so that the fabric fell from her waist in even pleats at the front and back, leaving the fabric at the top to drape down Jennifer's arms, almost like sleeves.

All of them wore their beaded pectoral collars, which extended halfway to their shoulders. Ramose's and Mentmose's black wigs were smooth and shiny, held down with narrow bands of gold. The dozens of braids, tied off with tiny beaded wires, that made up Meryt-Re's and Jennifer's wigs swayed gracefully with every movement of their heads.

Meryt-Re gestured for them all to turn, slowly.

"Now, the finishing touch," said Meryt-Re. "Mentmose, bring me my cosmetics table, please."

Mentmose ran up the stairs at a pace that made Meryt-Re wince, then returned carrying the spindly-legged table that Jennifer had seen sitting in the larger bedroom. Meryt-Re opened it and began expertly mixing powders from several jars with water on a stone palette. One at a time, they all sat in front of her, where she applied the dark kohl with quick strokes from a small stone spatula. She spent a little more time on Jennifer, highlighting her eyes with green and her cheeks with pink, and painting her lips.

Jennifer longed to scratch at the itchy make-up, but Meryt-Re scowled at her when she reached for her cheek. Meryt-Re handed her the bronze mirror, and gestured that she should look at herself. Why, she was beautiful! Meryt-Re had turned her into an elegant lady.

"I would hardly know you were my own daughter," said Ramose, chuckling.

"Uh," said Jennifer, swallowing. If they only knew how true that was!

With quick strokes, Meryt-Re put on her own make-up. And just in time, too.

There was a knock on the door, but before anyone could answer it, Tetisheri burst in, with a man and a woman following more sedately.

"Are you ready?" asked Tetisheri. She gazed at Mentmose. "You look wonderful!"

"Hello, Meryt-Re," said the woman, in a cool tone. She, too, was dressed in sheer linen and gold jewelry, though she wore a lot more than Meryt-Re. Too much, Jennifer thought, eyeing the woman's golden headband, earrings, bracelets, rings, and anklets.

"Hello, Satyah," said Meryt-Re. "Good evening, Hekhanakhte."

"Good evening." Tetisheri's father, also adorned with jewelry, gestured outside. "I have hired several con-veyances for us."

"You didn't have to do that," said Ramose. "We

167

could have walked."

"The second assistant official to the Curator of Monuments does not walk," said Satyah, with a sniff.

"Yes, you are quite right, Satyah," said Meryt-Re. "We thank you for your forethought and generosity."

"I've never ridden in a sedan chair before," said Tetisheri. Her cheeks turned pink as she turned to Mentmose. "Mentmose, would you like to share mine?"

Mentmose opened his mouth, but a glance from his mother quelled anything he was about to say. He gave Tetisheri a short, jerky nod.

"I thought the girls…" said Satyah.

"Please, mother?" said Tetisheri.

"I think that would be fine," said Meryt-Re. "Dje-Nefer can ride with us."

Satyah pursed her lips, but said nothing further.

The little cat that had slept with Jennifer the night before chose that moment to stalk regally into the room.

"Here is little Miw to bid us goodbye," said Tetisheri.

"Still only one cat, Meryt-Re?" asked Satyah, with a toss of her head. "We have three now. They were bred from the sacred temple cats."

"All cats are sacred, Satyah," said Meryt-Re. "Miw may not have had an exalted birth, but she is still beloved in the heart of Bastet. She does her job. We have not had any snakes in this house since we adopted her."

Miw rubbed up against Jennifer's legs and allowed herself to be lightly stroked. Then she wandered away, intent on her own mysterious feline errands.

"You should get another," said Satyah. "They are proof against demons, too, you know."

"So I've heard," said Meryt-Re. She opened the front door. "Shall we?"

Three painted and gilded boxy sedan chairs were lined up in front of the house. Several of the neighbors were peeking out from their front doors and peering down at the street from their roofs. Mentmose waved cheerfully at them all.

When they were all settled in their seats, the bearers started out at a steady walk, the lead man calling out the rhythm.

"Should we shut the curtains?" asked Ramose, his hand on a length of fabric that hung beside the windows.

Meryt-Re shook her head.

"No, I think not. We shall see and be seen. It is well that the world knows Ramose the amulet-maker and his family are on their way to the palace tonight. This will be an evening to remember."

Jennifer squirmed, trying to find a comfortable spot to sit on the palace's stone floor. She sneaked a peek at Meryt-Re, who was reclining on a pillow, fiddling with a tiny bird's drumstick. There was a faint crease between her eyebrows.

The feast had been going for hours, ever since they had arrived, and it didn't look like it was going to wind down any time soon. The narrow hall was filled with people. Young girls walked up and down the rows, offering food and wine.

All evening, groups and individuals had been brought forward to the front of the long room, for presentations to the Pharaoh or other business. Earlier, Meryt-Re had happily chatted with those around them, making sure to mention Mutemwija's name whenever she was asked about her outfit. Now, she barely spoke; she just kept glancing up at the Pharaoh's throne. It didn't help that they were at the very far end of the hall, only a few places removed from the exit.

Ka-Aper had sauntered by some time ago, barely

giving them a glance, followed by Neferhotep, who had seemed startled to see them there. They hadn't seen either of the men since.

"Would you like some sea slugs?" asked Ramose, holding out a bowl of quivering, jelly-like slices toward her.

"No, thank you," said Meryt-Re, her attention further up the room.

Ramose gave her a worried frown. He offered the slugs to Jennifer, who shook her head. "So…what do you think of your first feast?" he asked.

Jennifer shrugged. "It's all right."

Meryt-Re snorted but didn't say anything. Some of the food had been good, especially the chicken in a tangy sauce. There had even been a bowl of little cakes that had a marshmallow flavor. She had gobbled down as much of them as she thought she could get away with.

Jennifer hadn't been sure whether Dje-Nefer would have known what some of the dishes were, but Ramose and Meryt-Re hadn't been surprised at her questions. Meryt-Re had remarked on how some of the spices were rare and unusual, before their seatmates had laughed and told her their servants used them all the time.

Ramose handed Jennifer a red bowl, which was nearly empty. "More candy? They are truly a delicacy. The Pharaoh is quite generous to allow them to be served tonight. Usually, they are reserved for royalty."

With a glance at Meryt-Re, Jennifer plucked out the last two and nibbled on the sweet treat. At least they weren't slippery, like the heavily sauced meats, some of which Jennifer had nearly dropped on her new dress.

Meryt-Re was still staring up the room.

"Something wrong, dear heart?" asked Ramose.

"You know there is, Ramose," said Meryt-Re, sitting up. "Could we be any further away from the royal dais? Look at us! We are practically out in the hallway."

"Well, we couldn't expect…"

"Ramose."

"At least Mentmose is closer," said Ramose, a little desperately.

"Only because Tetisheri threatened to make a scene if he was not allowed to sit by her and her parents," said Meryt-Re. She threw the uneaten drumstick back into the communal bowl which they were sharing with another couple.

"Meryt-Re," said Ramose, "your voice…"

"Yes. I know. Keep it down. We would not want to seem ungrateful," said Meryt-Re. "But Ramose! Even Seneb the fish merchant has a closer position than we do. How he got invited, I would like to know."

"It looks like he came with a friend," said Ramose. He chuckled as he glanced at the fish vendor. "You'll note, not too many people are willing to sit beside him."

"I am not surprised. Gossip in the market is that his nose has never worked properly," said Meryt-Re. "Doubtless he does not realize that he could be mistaken for one of his catch."

"Meryt-Re, I'm sure there is a good reason for us being so far back. We were invited quite late, after all," said Ramose.

"I suppose. But we were invited. Specifically by Ka-Aper. He as good as promised that you would come to the Pharaoh's attention tonight, didn't he?" asked Meryt-Re.

"You must be patient," said Ramose. "Wait! Here comes Neferhotep."

They sat up straighter as Neferhotep neared them,

the head of his leopard skin bouncing on his bare chest with every long stride. He kneeled in front of them.

"Meryt-Re, Ramose, I didn't know you were going to be here. Ka-Aper told me earlier that he invited you, but he has kept me in attendance ever since the feast began, or I would have come to talk with you," he said, with a frown.

"What's the matter?" asked Ramose.

"I…nothing. Ka-Aper has asked for you to come forward now. The children, too," said Neferhotep. "Dje-Nefer, I think he wants you to show your amulet to the Pharaoh. He said there was something she needed to see."

"Should I bring my gifts for the Pharaoh, too?" asked Ramose, as he scooped up the bag that held the amulets he had brought for her.

"By all means," said Neferhotep.

Ramose rose and helped Meryt-Re to stand. Jennifer scrambled to her feet.

"Wait," said Meryt-Re. She twitched one of Ramose's pleats into more precise alignment and brushed a few crumbs from Jennifer's front. "All right. Let's go. We can pick up Mentmose on the way."

They filed up the long hall behind Neferhotep, Jennifer behind Ramose and Meryt-Re. As they passed Tetisheri's family, Satyah looked at them in astonishment. Meryt-Re crooked a finger at Mentmose. He popped up from the floor and followed them. Tetisheri made an attempt to join him, but her mother pulled her firmly back.

Jennifer tried to peer around Neferhotep, to see if she could spot the Pharaoh. After what felt like miles of walking, with every eye in the room on them, Neferhotep stopped suddenly and bowed. Jennifer and the others copied him. She peeked out from under the bangs of her wig to get a good look at the people on the dais.

A plump middle-aged woman, seated on a straight-backed golden throne, beckoned them forward. Her beaded pectoral collar reached to her shoulders, and her black hair had tiny gold disks braided into it. It was topped by a delicate golden crown, with a cobra and vulture at the front. Her outfit was similar to Meryt-Re's, although even from where she was standing, Jennifer could tell that the fabric was finer. It shone like silk in the light from the torches. Apparently, the Pharaoh didn't wear men's clothing all the time.

Behind her throne stood a giant of a man, his skin almost as dark as the black stone that Ramose often worked with. He stood silently behind the Pharaoh, his eyes closed and his bulging arms folded over his massive chest.

"You may speak," said the Pharaoh. Her voice was strong and pleasant, even friendly.

They straightened out of their bows and faced her. Neferhotep gestured grandly.

"Your Majesty, may I present Ramose the amulet-maker and his family," he said in ringing tones.

"Ka-Aper has mentioned you," said Hatshepsut.

Ramose's chest swelled with pride. Ka-Aper himself was standing to the right of Hatshepsut, smiling at them. His outfit was similar to the one he had worn to dinner at Ramose's house, but he had added even more jewelry. He even wore a cape, which swept down in soft folds from his wide shoulders all the way to the floor.

"An amulet-maker, Aunt?" drawled a young man, who lounged on a pillow at the Pharaoh's feet. It was the young man from the temple. "Are you in need of protection?"

"We can all use assistance, from time to time, Thutmose," said Hatshepsut. "Even you."

Thutmose smirked. "Of course. You are always right."

Neferhotep cleared his throat. "My brother makes the finest amulets in all of the Black Land. Most people prefer his over any others for their mummies."

"Is it so?" asked Hatshepsut. "I would like to see some."

Neferhotep nodded to Ramose, who stepped forward and bowed deeply again. "For your most gracious Majesty," he said, handing her the bag.

Thutmose snorted softly.

Hatshepsut's lips curved upwards as she opened the bag and poured the contents into her hand. "How delightful! Fine indeed," she said, as she examined a carnelian crocodile.

"He has created a most cunning amulet for his daughter, as well," said Ka-Aper.

Meryt-Re nudged Jennifer forward. She stepped

closer. As she bowed, the scarab amulet swung outward on its thong. When she looked at the Pharaoh again, Hatshepsut was smiling at her.

"Come closer, child," she said, in a gentle voice.

Jennifer climbed onto the low dais.

"May I see the amulet?" asked Hatshepsut.

Jennifer glanced at Ramose, who nodded. She lifted it over her head and handed it to the Pharaoh.

"It is lovely," said Hatshepsut.

Jennifer swallowed. She'd never have a better chance to mention the conspiracy. "Your Majesty…" she whispered.

"Yes? What is it, child?" the Pharaoh whispered back.

"I…I need to tell you something," said Jennifer.

Ka-Aper leaned towards them, his face so close she could feel his breath on her cheek.

Jennifer gulped. He grinned at her.

"The amulet opens, too. It's really quite clever," he said.

Jennifer gasped. The beads! If Hatshepsut opened it, they would fall out. Ka-Aper was right there. She didn't want him to see that she had them.

"Let me show you," said Jennifer. Hatshepsut handed the amulet back. Jennifer slid her nail into the crack and opened it a little. She curled her fist around the beads as they slid into her hand. Had Ka-Aper noticed? She handed the amulet back to the Pharaoh.

"Ah," said Hatshepsut, running her finger around the smooth interior, just as Jennifer had done. "Very nice."

"Perhaps you should consider giving it to the Pharaoh, child," Ka-Aper suggested.

Jennifer drew in a breath. But then how would she get home?

"No," said Hatshepsut, giving it back to Jennifer. "I think this young lady likes the gift her father made for her very much. It would not be right to take it away."

"Of course. It is very fine," said Ka-Aper. "May I take a closer look?"

Puzzled, Jennifer gave it to him. He had already seen it. Ka-Aper held it by the thong and let it dangle in front of his face as he inspected it.

"Was the amulet made for a particular purpose?" asked Hatshepsut.

"Just for my daughter's birth anniversary," said

Ramose, "but…" He glanced at Neferhotep.

"But it soon turned out to have a use," Ka-Aper completed the sentence.

"Oh?" said Hatshepsut.

"We…I…we feared that a demon might have tried to possess her," said Neferhotep. "The amulet should help protect her from them. When I am able to do so, I will put a special spell of herbs and perfumes in it, for extra security."

"A demon?" asked Hatshepsut, sitting back in her throne. Her voice was cool.

"Yes," said Neferhotep. "My niece fell asleep on her roof a few days ago. I had warded the garden against the Walkers of the Night, but when I checked, I found that the reeds had been pressed apart in one place. A demon could have entered there."

Jennifer heard Meryt-Re take a sharp breath, behind her.

"Had you evidence of any possession?" asked Hatshepsut.

"Well…" said Neferhotep.

"Come now," Ka-Aper interrupted. "You told me

yourself she had been acting oddly." He put his hand on Jennifer's shoulder. She wanted to squirm away from it, but he held her firm.

"Yes, but," Neferhotep began.

Ka-Aper, his hand still on Jennifer, turned them both to face the crowded hall and held the amulet high.

"Demons," he boomed. "They are everywhere. This amulet was meant to protect this beautiful child. But it is, I fear, too little, too late. Your Majesty, as a priest of Amon-Ra, I am able to detect such things. This girl has been possessed!"

"What?" said Neferhotep.

A ripple of surprise and fear surged through the crowd.

Meryt-Re gasped. Mentmose's mouth dropped open. Ramose started forward, but stopped when Ka-Aper pointed at them.

"I call these good people to witness. Can you assure me that your daughter has been acting like herself lately?" asked Ka-Aper.

All three of them hesitated.

"Can you?" Ka-Aper snapped. "Swear on the feather

of Ma'at! For if you lie, you know that your hearts will be in peril."

Meryt-Re put a hand over her chest and breathed hard. Tears welled up in her eyes. Mentmose looked at the floor, no doubt remembering how he had found her on the roof after she'd been told not to go there. And her reaction to the hippopotamus. Ramose lowered his eyes, too.

Even Neferhotep didn't meet Jennifer's gaze. He was watching Ka-Aper.

Jennifer opened her mouth. This was silly!

"Do not speak, demon," said Ka-Aper, giving her a shake.

"This is a serious accusation," Hatshepsut drawled from behind them.

Ka-Aper turned back to face her, Jennifer still in his iron grip. A slow, ugly smile spread across his face, one that she did not like at all.

"These are serious times," he said softly. "Demons walk the night and are not stopped from possessing its people. This did not happen in your father's time. It is an indication of how far Kemet, the Black Land, has fallen."

The smile on Hatshepsut' lips did not reach her eyes. "I see. And what is it you suggest we do?"

"Why, we must do what we always do with demons," said Ka-Aper. "We must drive it out of her body."

"As I recall, the last time you tried that, you weren't satisfied that your exorcism had worked," said Hatshepsut. "The girl died."

"Sometimes that happens," said Ka-Aper.

"No!" Meryt-Re choked out. "Not my daughter!"

"Woman, she is not your daughter," said Ka-Aper. "We will do what we can. It may not be enough."

"I don't understand," said Ramose. "The amulet is proof against demons, and she has been wearing it…"

"Perhaps you were not as precise in your carving as you thought," said Ka-Aper. "Or perhaps this is a very strong demon, drawn to our country in its…weakness."

"I see," Hatshepsut said again, tapping her fingers on the arm of her throne. "Truly I do." The black man behind the Pharaoh's throne shifted slightly to the right.

Ka-Aper pointed at one of the soldiers who guarded the dais. "Come here! Take this girl away and put her in a cell."

The guard hesitated, looking not at Hatshepsut, but at Thutmose, who slowly nodded. Catching this, Hatshepsut's eyes narrowed. The soldier slipped a short sword out of the scabbard at his hip and advanced on Jennifer.

"No!" Meryt-Re wailed, pulling on Ka-Aper's arm. "Please!"

Ka-Aper's hand slipped off Jennifer's shoulder as he shoved Meryt-Re back into Ramose's embrace. He whirled and reached for Jennifer again.

She had to get out of here. If she ended up in one of the cells, she would probably never see daylight again. She whipped her gaze around her, looking for a place to escape. There! She could see an open doorway behind the black man. Jennifer dived past him. He reached for her, but amazingly, she slipped through his grasp and was off, running for the exit. A roar of anger followed her.

She ducked through the door and found herself in an empty, torch-lit hall which branched off in several directions. She picked one at random and pelted down it, skidding around the corners.

At Satyah's request, a palace servant had given them a short tour of the palace, before the feast, but they had taken so many twists and turns in the huge stone building to get to the banquet hall that she had no idea where she was. She trotted down the narrow corridor, which opened into a much larger one. Faint cries of pursuit followed her, spurring her to greater speed. She needed to find a way out of the palace. At least there was no one around to stop her.

Jennifer ran around another corner, her sandals slapping against the sand-coated floor, and slammed into someone. Both of them fell in a jumble of tangling limbs. Jennifer's hand jerked open, and the beads bounced away.

"Ooof," said the person Jennifer had run into.

Jennifer struggled to get away, then caught sight of the woman's face.

"Mutemwija!" she said, helping her to rise. "What are you doing here?"

The old woman from the market was breathing heavily, her clothes twisted and her gray hair mussed. Food and other items had sprayed out of a black fabric bag that spun across the floor. She put a hand on her head and laughed. "Good thing I'm well-padded. Jennifer, you sure pack a wallop!"

Jennifer sat back on her haunches, hard.

"Jennifer?" said the woman. "Are you all right, dear?"

"Mutemwija?"

"Not today, Jennifer."

"G-g-grandma Jo?" said Jennifer. "Is it you?"

"Of course, dear," she said. A shout, echoing down the corridor, interrupted her. "What's going on?"

Jennifer glanced over her shoulder. "They're after me."

"Who's after you?" asked Grandma Jo, stuffing the dropped items into a shapeless black bag, much like the one she carried in their own time. The sight of it convinced Jennifer that this really was Grandma Jo.

"Uh, some soldiers. And a priest."

"What?"

"Never mind. We have to get out of here," said Jennifer. She grabbed her grandmother's hand. "Come on!"

"Oooh," said Grandma Jo, taking a step.

"What's wrong?"

"I'm not sure I can walk," said Grandma Jo, massaging her leg. "I think I may have twisted something, when you plowed into me."

"Oh, no," said Jennifer. "We'll have to hide some-where while you rest up."

She padded down the hall, Grandma Jo limping beside her. The sound of running feet was getting clos-er, and she thought she heard a familiar voice. Sound bounced off the walls, distorting the echoes.

Jennifer spotted a darkened doorway.

"Quick! In here," she whispered, pulling her grand-mother through into the shadows.

"Where are we?" asked Grandma Jo.

"No idea," said Jennifer, one hand outstretched to feel her way along the wall. She cracked her shin against something large and hard. "Ow!"

"What is it?"

Jennifer fingered the round clay vessel, which was tightly stoppered and sealed with wax. "I think it's a big jar."

As her eyes adjusted to the darkness, she could see that the room was full of dozens of them, all about the size of a basketball. There were stacks of them close to one wall.

"We can hide behind these," she said. She led Grandma Jo over to the stack.

"Ugh," said Grandma Jo. "I've stepped in something sticky."

Jennifer realized that her sandals were making a sucking sound on the floor. She must have stepped in it too.

Grandma Jo felt at the floor, then sniffed her fingers. "It smells sharp and bitter. And familiar."

Jennifer sniffed. It did smell familiar. Like…

"The amulet! Grandma, this smells like the stuff that was in my amulet!"

"My goodness, you're right," said Grandma Jo. "Maybe that's what sent us here."

"What? You mean you…"

"Well, of course, dear. How else do you think I got here?" said Grandma Jo. "Poor Dje-Nefer. She was very confused. And scared. So was I, until I figured out what had happened."

"So I was right?" asked Jennifer. "We did switch bodies?"

"I think so. After you—she—fainted in the car, I

brought you, um, her back to my place. When she woke up, she was babbling. It took me a while to realize that it wasn't just you doing a really good acting job. The things she said convinced me."

"Why didn't you send Dje-Nefer back with the dust?" asked Jennifer.

"We tried. But nothing happened. So I tried it instead. I didn't know if it would work. Anyway, I had to try. I couldn't just leave you here alone."

Jennifer smiled. She had to admit it felt good to have Grandma Jo with her.

"Then Mutemwija's in your body now? Is that going to be a problem?" she asked.

"I hope not. Anyway, I left Harriet in charge. I told her I had something much more interesting than bingo for her to do," said Grandma Jo. "She may not have believed me, but she was willing to go along with it. I'm sure she's coping with both of them. She's unflappable."

"Do you think Harriet will try to time travel, too?"

"She can't. There was only a tiny bit of dust left in the amulet. It would have been all gone after I...left. And found myself here."

"In Ancient Egypt," said Jennifer.

"Yes. I was kind of expecting it, after what happened to you, but it still caught me by surprise. I panicked when I woke up in Mutemwija's body. Her grandson was not amused."

"So that was you, in the market," said Jennifer. "Didn't you recognize me?"

"Of course I did. But I couldn't very well say anything in front of Meryt-Re, could I? I realized she had no idea of who you really were, and I didn't want to give you away."

"I haven't told her, or anyone, who I am," said Jennifer.

"That's probably wise," said Grandma Jo.

"Do Mom and Dad know? About the time travel?" asked Jennifer.

"No," said Grandma Jo. "I didn't want to worry them. I just asked your mother if she minded me keeping you for a weekend sleepover."

"What day is it? Back home, I mean?" asked Jennifer.

"I'm not sure. It might be Monday," said Grandma

Jo. Jennifer gasped. "But don't worry. It's a holiday, remember?"

"Oh, yeah. But what will happen if I don't get back home before Dje-Nefer has to go to school for me?" asked Jennifer.

"Harriet will think of something," said Grandma Jo. "Meanwhile, we need to think of a way to get out of this situation. What's going on?"

"It's...complicated. But there's a guy who thinks I'm a demon," said Jennifer.

"A what?"

"Ssh," said Jennifer. Someone was coming. They ducked behind the stack of pots.

"Try that way," said a man, his voice rebounding off the walls.

"All right," said another. "But she could be anywhere by now."

Jennifer sucked in a breath. It was the same voice she had heard in the warehouse basement, where she had found the beads.

She stiffened. The beads! They were probably still in the corridor where she had dropped them when she and

Grandma Jo had collided.

The voices drifted away down the hall. Jennifer inched her way back to the open door of the storage room.

"Where are you going?" asked Grandma Jo.

"I have to get something," said Jennifer. "It's important."

As she reached the door, she heard someone coming again and flattened herself against the wall inside the room. The person peeked inside, light from the torch he held high throwing the room's furnishings into view. His face was in shadow. He looked around carefully, then hesitated, staring at the floor. He lifted his gaze and stared intently at the pile of stacked jars where Grandma Jo was hiding. Beyond it, Jennifer could see the dark slash of another exit. Jennifer waited, breathing silently through her nose, expecting him to enter at any moment.

Instead he withdrew, apparently satisfied that the room was empty, and kept going down the hall, taking the light with him. Jennifer cautiously peered around the wall, to see the back of a bald-headed man, as he strode away under the flickering torchlight. Ka-Aper? He turned his head slightly, and she recognized him. Not Ka-Aper. Neferhotep!

Was he one of the tomb robbers, too? Jennifer shook her head. She hadn't wanted it to be him.

She quickly ran down the corridor, but couldn't spot the glitter of the beads. Where were they? It sounded like Neferhotep was coming back. Maybe he'd seen her and Grandma Jo after all. Jennifer whisked back to where Grandma Jo was hiding, slumped against the wall.

"We have to get out of here," she said.

"Sweetheart, I can't. I think my ankle is sprained," said Grandma Jo.

"I'll help you," said Jennifer. "There's a door at the end."

With Jennifer supporting her, they limped over to the door and slipped through. Jennifer gave the storage room a last glance over her shoulder. Her eyes widened. There, in plain sight on the floor and illuminated by the light from the corridor, were their footprints. They had tracked sand in on their sandals and left it in the sticky puddle in perfect outlines.

Neferhotep must have seen the footprints when he looked in the storage room. But why had he left again, then? Maybe to get Ka-Aper! She walked a little faster, pulling Grandma Jo along as quickly as she dared, reaching out with her other hand to feel her way in the pitch blackness. Soon, she encountered another wall, but it opened into another room. She stepped out into it, feeling somehow that this was a much larger space.

A strong, warm hand clamped around her wrist. Jennifer screamed.

"What? What is it?" asked Grandma Jo.

"Ssh, you must be quiet," someone rumbled.

"K-K-Ka-Aper?" said Jennifer.

The man chuckled. "No. You have not such luck."

"Who are you?" asked Grandma Jo.

"No one important. And no one you must fear. But you must come with me." He tugged on Jennifer's arm, and Grandma Jo staggered against her with a cry.

"Wait," he said. "You are hurt?"

"My grandm— my friend is," said Jennifer.

"I see." He released Jennifer and gently probed along her shoulder, finding Grandma Jo's arm held tight around it. "What is hurting?"

"My ankle," said Grandma Jo.

"Let me help," said the man. He took Grandma Jo

from Jennifer. She couldn't see what he was doing, but something made Grandma Jo gasp.

"Grandma? Uh, Mutemwija?"

"It's all right. He's carrying me over his shoulder," said Grandma Jo.

"Oh." Jennifer was torn. She wanted to run from this strange man. But he had Grandma Jo. She couldn't leave her.

"Come with me," he said again. "Someone wishes to speak with you."

"Who?"

"Someone who wishes you no ill. Now, you must be silent."

She felt, rather than heard him move away. His steps were silent on the stone floor. No matter how quiet Jennifer tried to be, her sandals made squeaking sounds. She finally slipped them off, and jogged to catch up with him.

He led them through several of the storage rooms, some filled with objects, which he carefully navigated around. After she stubbed a toe on something, he reached out and held her hand in his own, leading them further and further away from their pursuers. How he could see so well in such deep darkness, she didn't know.

At last, they seemed to have finished threading their way through the maze of storage rooms. Jennifer wasn't sure, but she thought they were deep within the palace. Faint light beckoned to them from an arched doorway. He led them through it, and Jennifer felt fresh, cool air whispering against her skin, scented with the aroma of green, growing things. She looked up. Stars twinkled overhead, real ones, not just paintings on a ceiling.

Jennifer took a deep breath, heavy with moisture. Large, tree-shaped shadows loomed over a pebbled path. Jennifer let go of the man's hand and followed him as he led her into a fragrant jungle of trees and bushes. The faint drip and trickle of water grew louder as they ducked under leaves, following the path. It led to a small clearing, and now Jennifer could make out a wall behind it, dotted here and there with small torches.

Tall plants with long stems and hairy tops lined the edges of a small rectangular pool in the middle of the clearing, its surface broken by flat leaves like lily pads, with small flowers.

"Where are we?" asked Grandma Jo. The black man didn't answer.

"I don't know," said Jennifer.

The man lowered Grandma Jo to the ground. She landed on her sore leg with a grunt.

"Are you all right, Grandma?" asked Jennifer.

"I'm fine, dear," she said. "Just sore. I'll be better in a little while."

"I wonder who this garden belongs to," said Jennifer.

"It belongs to the Pharaoh."

"How do you know?" asked Jennifer.

"Um, Jennifer dear, that wasn't me speaking," said Grandma Jo.

"Then who…"

"It was I."

Jennifer whirled, trying to place the source of the soft, pleasant voice. A white shape came into focus as she peered into the gloom under the trees. A woman was sitting on a stone bench, her hands folded in her lap.

"Welcome," said Hatshepsut.

"Please," said the Pharaoh, "be seated." She gestured at a stone bench near hers.

Grandma Jo bowed, then sat down. "Your Majesty."

Belatedly, Jennifer dipped her head in a jerky curtsey.

Hatshepsut laughed. "You needn't stand on ceremony here, my dears. Come, sit. Dje-Nefer, isn't it? Such a pretty name. Who is this with you? Your grandmother, you said?"

"It's just a term of respect," Grandma Jo said hastily.

"I see," said Hatshepsut.

"This is a beautiful place," said Grandma Jo. Jennifer gingerly sat next to her on the bench. Grandma Jo settled her black bag on the ground, then took one of Jennifer's hands and held it. Jennifer held back, hard.

"Thank you. It's my favorite courtyard," said Hatshepsut. The Pharaoh picked up a piece of bread from beside her. "Excuse me. I can never eat at the feasts, with so many people watching my every move. Do you mind?"

"No, of course not," said Grandma Jo.

Hatshepsut bit down on the bread. "Ow!" she said, wincing. "I shall have to have that tooth removed."

"Are you going to arrest us?" Jennifer blurted.

"Arrest you? Whatever for?" Hatshepsut prodded at her cheek with one plump hand.

"Because—because—don't you think I'm a demon?" asked Jennifer. "Ka-Aper does."

Hatshepsut shook her head, making the tiny disks in her hair tinkle. "Ah, Ka-Aper. He is one who sees demons everywhere. I do not believe in them. But of course, I cannot let that be known in front of my people. They would be shocked."

"So you had to pretend to agree with him?" asked Jennifer.

"Yes." Hatshepsut sighed. "Unfortunately, the last time he claimed that someone was possessed by a demon, I was unable to save the child. Bibi knows how much I regret that." She nodded towards the man who had carried Grandma Jo. He had withdrawn from them and now stood back in the shadows, with his arms once more folded across his broad chest.

"We know who the real demons are," he said.

"You do?" said Jennifer.

Hatshepsut chuckled. "Do not be afraid. We have never seen a demon, though others say they exist. Bibi refers to those misguided people who enjoy frightening children. Ka-Aper is one of them, as you have found out. He was not always this way. I remember a time when he was open-minded and more inclined to philosophy and research. He was a staunch supporter when I took the throne. Now, he has joined the ranks of those who oppose my policies, in the name of 'doing what's right for the people.' There are even some of those who seek my death."

"Well, uh, Ka-Aper is one of them," said Jennifer.

"Oh, I do not think he would be so bold as to attack me."

"Maybe not, but he could get someone else to do it," said Jennifer. She leaned forward. "Which I think he did. I heard him."

"You did? How?" asked Hatshepsut.

"I followed him. He went into the basement of a warehouse and met with some men. Tomb robbers!"

"Tomb robbers?" Hatshepsut's head snapped up. "So.

202

Ka-Aper now stoops as low as that. I did not know."

"He said they had a map to someone's tomb. He also gave them a package that I saw him get from a house near ours. I think it had some sort of poison in it. Then he said that when the Pharaoh was dead, he would act as surprised as everyone else."

"He truly intends my death? That puts a new face on the situation," said Hatshepsut. "His little conspiracy has grown fangs."

"You mean, you knew about it?" asked Jennifer.

The Pharaoh sighed. "My earthly father was a good man, but even he had to combat the occasional conspiracy against him. I learned from him to be wary. I have spies in the city—in the market, in the streets, and yes, even in the temple. In all my twenty years on the throne, I have managed to thwart several conspiracies. I knew Ka-Aper was up to something, but not what, exactly. Nor do I know who his co-conspirators are. If I could find one, he might be persuaded to expose Ka-Aper."

"I think I know who Ka-Aper's friends are," said Jennifer. "Or at least one of them."

"Who might that be?" asked Hatshepsut.

Jennifer hung her head. She didn't want to say it.

"Come, child, you must tell me."

"N-Neferhotep," Jennifer stutterd. "He's a priest of Amon-Ra, and Ramose...m-my father's...brother."

"Ah," said Hatshepsut. "Why do you think he is part of the conspiracy?"

"Neferhotep believes in demons. He had the map for the tomb robbers, which Ka-Aper now has. And when I ran away from Ka-Aper—did I tell you, he nearly caught me?—Neferhotep found me. He was breathing hard, like he'd been running. Chasing me, maybe." She took a deep breath. "Then when we were hiding, here in the palace, I looked out and saw him."

Hatshepsut nodded. "I know. I sent him after you this evening."

"You sent him?" said Jennifer.

"Yes. Just as I sent him after Ka-Aper that day. After you...escaped...from us tonight, Ka-Aper sent guards and others to find you. I asked Neferhotep to follow you, to make sure that they did not succeed."

"You mean...he's on your side?" asked Jennifer.

"Yes," said Hatshepsut, "and has been for some time.

He, too, suspected Ka-Aper of some untoward dealings. He came to me."

"I couldn't find any proof, though," said Neferhotep, as he came striding through the bushes. He smiled at Jennifer and bowed to the Pharaoh. "Ka-Aper is very clever."

"But I thought," Jennifer began.

"I told you I had spies everywhere, even the temple," said Hatshepsut. "You shouldn't suspect your own uncle, child. I think your grandmother would tell you that."

"Grandmother?" asked Neferhotep, as he sat cross-legged on the ground by the Pharaoh. He looked expectantly at Jennifer. "Dje-Nefer, your grandmothers are both deceased."

"Oh! This is G-, I mean Mutemwija. Of course you know she isn't really my grandmother. I just call her that. We met her in the market. She's the one who made our outfits," said Jennifer, plucking at the fabric of her dress.

"I am honored to meet you," said Neferhotep.

"Thank you," said Grandma Jo. "It's an honor to meet you, too."

"You came to the feast with Dje-Nefer, then?"

"No," said Grandma Jo. "Actually, I sneaked in. I told a nice young soldier that I had a cousin in the kitchens whom I wanted to visit, and he let me pass. He was a sweetie."

"Wow, really? That doesn't sound like most of the soldiers I've seen," said Jennifer.

"What do you mean?" asked Hatshepsut.

"I saw some of them taking 'traitors' away, when I first got…uh, one day," said Jennifer. "They were pretty rough."

"What? My soldiers have no orders to do that," said Hatshepsut.

"Perhaps they are following someone else's orders," said Neferhotep. "One who thinks soldiers have better things to do than break up arguments in the marketplaces."

"My army is only for peacekeeping and defense," said Hatshepsut. "I do not believe in making war upon my neighbors."

Neferhotep cleared his throat. "There are those who believe otherwise."

"You mean my nephew. I know," said Hatshepsut, "that he would prefer glory. But I have him safe under the priests' eyes at the moment, where he cannot make too much trouble."

"Maybe," said Jennifer, remembering how the soldiers had looked to Prince Thutmose for permission to take her away. "Ka-Aper is a priest."

Hatshepsut was silent for a moment. "That is true."

"In any case, I still need the proof that Ka-Aper is involved in this particular conspiracy," said Neferhotep. "After Dje-Nefer and Tetisheri visited me in the temple, I followed Ka-Aper to what I suspected might be a meeting. I think he knew I was following him. He lost me in a market."

"I followed him, too," said Jennifer.

"You did?" asked Neferhotep. "That was dangerous."

"She has already proven that she is a brave child," said Hatshepsut.

Neferhotep smiled. "I know. Did you discover anything, Dje-Nefer?"

"Yes," said Jennifer. "I thought he could lead me back to the temple, but instead, he went to a deserted warehouse."

"The warehouse! Of course," said Neferhotep.

"I was curious, so I went in after him and listened to them talking. There were three of them, Ka-Aper and two others," said Jennifer. "I thought you might have been one of them."

"Me!"

"You did find me right after that."

"I saw you go by, so I abandoned my search for Ka-Aper and ran after you," said Neferhotep. He turned to the Pharaoh. "It wasn't a very nice neighborhood. I had to look after my niece."

"Of course," Hatshepsut murmured.

"I thought that Ka-Aper had sent you after me," said Jennifer. "I even thought you were going to take me to him. He showed up at our door right after that."

"To invite you to the feast. I didn't know you'd been invited until he told me. I wondered why."

"He said he wanted to present Ramose to the Pharaoh," said Jennifer.

"I think he had a different intent in mind," said Hatshepsut. "He would like to see my utter destruction, would he not, Bibi?"

"Yes," said Bibi, still standing behind her. "He accuses people of being possessed by demons so that the populace will think the gods have abandoned us."

"He knows that I still have soldiers and priests loyal to me, so he does not dare attack me. Not yet," said Hatshepsut. "Though I begin to wonder what my nephew is planning."

"He still feels that you stole the crown from him, your Majesty," said Neferhotep, in a low voice.

Hatshepsut nodded. "I know."

"What else could you do?" asked Jennifer. "He was only a baby when your brother died."

"It has been a good reign, Majesty. We have had peace and prosperity for twenty years," said Neferhotep. "You have made trade treaties with other countries, and you have built beautiful monuments."

"Thanks to my faithful friend Senmut," said Hatshepsut.

"We all mourn the day he died," said Neferhotep. "He was a good man."

"It is only recently that things have begun to go badly," said Hatshepsut. "I became Pharaoh because I thought it was the right thing to do."

"Amon-Ra himself sanctioned it," said Neferhotep. "He inhabited your father's body and your mother later gave birth to you. He is your true father."

"Many do not believe it," said Hatshepsut.

"Ka-Aper and his friends sure don't," said Jennifer. "They said your reign was blash...blas...something."

"Blasphemous?" asked Hatshepsut. "That it goes against the gods' wishes?"

"Yes, and that's why you're having a drought," said Jennifer.

"Always, he seeks a means to undermine my authority," said Hatshepsut, pounding her fist into the bench. "Even if he must find demons under every rock to do it."

Neferhotep nodded. "Even now. He still has guards out looking for Dje-Nefer. Don't worry, niece, the rest of your family is safe. I brought them to one of your rooms, your Majesty, before I went searching for Dje-Nefer myself. A good thing, too, or they might have been pressed into service to look for you. Some of the guests were. I met one of them just before I found your hiding place."

"You knew where we were?" asked Jennifer.

"I saw your footprints," said Neferhotep. "I went to

report that you weren't in that corridor. But when I came back, you were gone."

"I found them," said Bibi. "I brought them to my Pharaoh."

"Footprints?" asked Grandma Jo. "You didn't tell me we'd left them, Jen."

"In the sticky puddle. Remember?"

"Yes, I'm afraid one of your jars of myrrh must have a leak, your Majesty," said Neferhotep.

"Myrrh!" said Jennifer.

"It is my favorite scent," said Hatshepsut. "I use it for almost everything."

Jennifer and Grandma Jo exchanged glances.

Neferhotep chuckled. "I wish the fellow I met in the hall had made use of it. I sent him off in a different direction so I didn't have to smell him anymore. He reeked of fish."

"Fish?" said Jennifer. "Seneb sells fish in the market. Meryt-Re buys from him."

"I remember now," said Neferhotep. "She mentioned him once."

"Wait," said Jennifer. "Meryt-Re said his nose didn't

work right. The man in the warehouse said he couldn't tell if the wine was any good, because he couldn't smell it! It's Seneb!"

"A fish merchant?" said Hatshepsut, in a wondering tone. "One of the tomb robbers? If this is true, then Ka-Aper has certainly found some unusual friends."

"Meryt-Re called him a pirate," said Jennifer.

The Pharaoh sat back on her bench and thought for a moment. Then she rose. "Come," she said, turning and heading away from the pool in the courtyard.

They all followed, Bibi supporting Grandma Jo with an arm under her shoulders. Pebbles crunched under their feet as they pushed past the fragrant branches of the trees. The path they followed ended near a doorway. Hatshepsut stepped through it and beckoned the others forward, into a room filled with light from dozens of oil lamps. Jennifer blinked in the sudden brightness.

Hatshepsut gracefully crossed the room, her san-daled feet skimming the tiled floor. She perched on a square golden chair, resting her elbows on its flat arms, her fingers curled over the snarling leopards' heads that decorated the ends. She nodded at several nearby benches and chairs. Bibi eased Grandma Jo down to a seat, feeling for it with his outstretched fingers, still with his eyes closed. With a start, Jennifer realized that he was blind.

"Bring this Seneb to me," Hatshepsut instructed Bibi. He nodded and left through the same door that the servants had used. "Neferhotep, do you think you could convince Ka-Aper to attend as well?"

"I think he still trusts me," said Neferhotep. "I have taken pains to assure him I know nothing of politics."

"Good. We will see what he says when we tell him we know about his…business," said Hatshepsut.

Neferhotep followed Bibi. Jennifer and Grandma Jo sat in silence with Hatshepsut. Grandma Jo rummaged in her black bag, then wiped her face on a scrap of linen that she'd found. She squinted at something that had fallen out with the linen, then shrugged and dropped it back in.

The Pharaoh waited patiently, not even tapping her fingers on the chair arms. She could have been one of her own statues.

Jennifer sat back and looked around the room. A

few small representations of the Pharaoh, some in men's clothing, and some in women's, stood on tables and cluttered shelves around the richly-decorated room. The furniture, strewn about in various places, was delicate and graceful, most of it painted gold.

One corner held a short cupboard, its doors painted with representations of the gods. On top, Jennifer recognized the red and white double crown of Upper and Lower Egypt, resting in splendid isolation. The image of a man wearing a split white crown was painted on the wall above the cupboard. Jennifer remembered him from the museum—Amon-Ra, the city-god of Thebes. A naked baby, one finger in its mouth, stared up at him.

Hatshepsut was watching Jennifer, an amused smile on her face.

"You are wondering if Amon-Ra truly is my father. When my father died, my brother Thutmose the Second became Pharaoh, even though he was only the son of my father's second wife. I became Great Royal Queen," said Hatshepsut. She smiled sadly. "When Thutmose died, many bureaucrats and officials immediately began to think they could gain power. I had to take steps or my country might have suffered from their greed."

"So you claimed the crown for yourself," said Grandma Jo.

"There was much opposition to it." Hatshepsut sighed. "I did have some support. My good friend Senmut. Some officials, some priests. Even Ka-Aper—then. I know my action was not popular. Then, one night Amon-Ra came to me in a dream. He said I was his daughter."

"Really?" asked Jennifer. "His daughter?"

"Yes! Of course, all Pharaohs are children to the gods, as Horus was to Osiris and Isis," said Hatshepsut. "So as daughter to Thutmose the First, and to the god Amon-Ra, I was therefore doubly suited to sit on the throne, even though I am a woman. I am the female Horus."

"Was it really Amon-Ra?"

"I do not know. But sometimes, late at night, I have glimpsed a man, in a white kilt and headdress, glowing with life…well. I cannot say." Hatshepsut leaned back in her chair, her gaze focused on something beyond the wall.

"Did you really wear men's clothing?" asked Jennifer,

peering at one of the small statues.

"Indeed I did," said Hatshepsut. "Only a few times, when I was much younger. There were many who said they wanted a man to reign. So I obliged them. It amused me greatly to dress like one—fake beard, short kilt, a man's headdress, and all. My enemies found it discomfiting. It also shut them up. It was most satisfactory."

There was a noise from the corridor outside the room. Jennifer heard voices, but couldn't make out the words.

"Ah," said Hatshepsut, with a grim smile.

Ka-Aper burst into the room, his cape swirling behind him, followed by Neferhotep and a couple of guards. Ka-Aper stopped talking when he saw Hatshepsut. His gaze skipped between her and Jennifer, and his eyes narrowed. Finally, he smiled and bowed.

"Your Majesty!" he said. "You've found the demon! Well done."

"Actually, it was my loyal servant Bibi who succeeded," said Hatshepsut. "He brought her to me."

"This is a temple matter. He should have brought her to us," said Ka-Aper. He gestured at Neferhotep, who had stepped back a few paces.

The two guards stood on either side of Ka-Aper, their hands on their sword hilts. Hatshepsut looked at them and then at Neferhotep, who nodded.

"Seize him!" she ordered.

The two guards drew their short swords and gripped Ka-Aper's arms. He struggled briefly, but couldn't break their hold.

"Unhand me!" he shouted.

"These guards are loyal to the Pharaoh," said Neferhotep. "My Lord Ka-Aper, you are under arrest."

"Don't be ridiculous," he said. "What for?"

"For treason," said Hatshepsut. "For conspiring to end my life. And for tomb robbing."

Ka-Aper's painted eyebrows rose. "Another conspiracy? You have stopped many during your reign, have you not? Real or imaginary! Are you now suspecting even the priests of Amon-Ra—your father?"

"No man is immune to the desire for power—not even a priest," said Hatshepsut.

Ka-Aper's face looked as though he had a clever idea. "Your Majesty," he purred, "it is easy to see that this demon girl has clouded your mind. You are not thinking clearly."

"I am thinking clearly, thank you," said Hatshepsut. "You were heard plotting with your friends to kill me. We know who at least one of your co-conspirators is."

"Who might that be?"

"Seneb, the fish merchant," said Hatshepsut.

Ka-Aper laughed. "Why would I consort with a seller of fish? The idea is preposterous."

"I agree," said Hatshepsut, "but we will ask the man himself. If I am not mistaken, here he comes now."

Jennifer looked towards the doorway. Sure enough, Bibi was entering with a man, his skinny arm clamped in one of Bibi's large, muscular hands. Jennifer wrinkled her nose as he drew nearer. It was Seneb, all right, despite the fact that he was dressed better than she'd seen him in the market. He wore gold jewelry and an intricately pleated white kilt. A lumpy leather pouch dangled from a strap slung crosswise over his chest. The smell of fish wafted from him, making Grandma Jo wrinkle her nose. Seneb's gaze darted from Ka-Aper to the Pharaoh and back again.

"Who is this?" asked Ka-Aper.

"Why, it is Seneb the fish merchant," said Hatshepsut. "Do you not know each other?"

"I have never seen this man in my life," said Ka-Aper.

"Seneb? Is this true?" asked Hatshepsut.

"I...," said Seneb, licking his lips. "O-of course." He chuckled nervously. "Why would Ka-Aper know a simple fish merchant like me?"

"Yet you know his name," said Hatshepsut.

"Of course," said Seneb, with a weak chuckle. "Wh-who doesn't know the famous Ka-Aper, priest of Amon-Ra?"

Hatshepsut stared at him. "Very well. Bibi, take him away. You know what to do with him."

Seneb glanced up at Bibi, who grinned.

"Yes, your Majesty," he said, starting to drag Seneb from the room.

"No! Wait!" said Seneb. "I do know him. He knows me! We've, uh, had some business together."

Ka-Aper hissed in frustration.

"Like tomb robbing?" asked Hatshepsut.

"How did you know...I mean, no, of course not,"

said Seneb. "Not tomb robbing."

"Liar," said Hatshepsut. "You were heard, speaking together. And then you were identified."

Seneb glanced at Neferhotep, sneering. "You? Kai said—"

"Kai?" said Neferhotep. "The temple priest?"

Jennifer remembered him—the one who had tried to take the amulets from her.

"Don't be a fool," said Ka-Aper. "Neferhotep did not hear anyone."

"Then who…" Seneb began. "The intruder! The one you chased…"

"I chased no one. I was not anywhere that I could chase an intruder," said Ka-Aper, with a meaningful look at Seneb. "It is, I think, this child who claims to have heard you. This demon child."

Seneb's look of fright turned thoughtful. A slow smile spread across his face. "A mere child. One who is accused of being a demon. Who would believe her?"

"I believe her," said Neferhotep.

Ka-Aper whirled on him, then bared his teeth. "Neferhotep, I knew there was something about you I didn't trust. You have always been one of the Pharaoh's supporters."

"Pharaoh Hatshepsut belongs on the throne," said Neferhotep, his chin lifting. "She has the right, and she has proved it over the years."

"Even if the gods have abandoned our country now?" asked Ka-Aper.

"They have not abandoned us!" said Hatshepsut.

Ka-Aper crossed his arms over his chest. "Your people are suffering, O Pharaoh. Do you not know? For seven long years, the Nile's great inundation has not flooded the Black Land as it should. Without the water, and the life-giving black mud that the river deposits, the soil has become dry and dead. No crops grow. The cattle go hungry. So do the people."

"There is still grain stored away," said Hatshepsut. "My people can still make bread."

"Those reserves are becoming low. One more poor year will do it," said Ka-Aper. "The granaries will be empty. Then what will you do?"

"The flood will come again," said Hatshepsut. "This is but a test of our faith. In the meantime, we can trade."

"With what?" asked Ka-Aper. "Your 'peaceful' reign has brought us no gold from other lands with which to trade for imported foods."

"Kemet will survive," said Hatshepsut. "We always have. I am and will be its Pharaoh."

"Not if the people have their say, O Great Queen," said Ka-Aper.

"Do not call me that," said Hatshepsut.

"Why not? It is your rightful title," said Ka-Aper. "The people will side with me. They are worried. Especially since demons like this girl abound in your land."

"You think her exorcism will appease them?" asked Neferhotep.

"No, not her exorcism," said Ka-Aper, grinning at him. "Her death."

Jennifer clenched her fists.

"Her death!" said Neferhotep. "You can't kill her!"

"Frankly, I do not care if she lives or dies," said Ka-Aper. "The threat is what matters."

"I don't understand," said Neferhotep.

"I think I do," said Hatshepsut. "If I prevent this child's death, my officials will be convinced that this demon has influenced me, which will prove me weak and untrustworthy. Since I will have shown such poor judgment in befriending this abomination, they will demand that I step down."

"As you know you should," said Ka-Aper. "You were never meant to be on the throne."

"If I do allow her death, then the people will think me a cruel ruler, a killer of children," said Hatshepsut. "The outcome would be the same."

"After which, you would take your own life," said Ka-Aper. "Out of grief."

"By what method?"

"Poison, of course," said Ka-Aper.

"A cowardly way to die," said Hatshepsut.

"Just so."

"Either way, Thutmose ends up on the throne," said Hatshepsut. "You, no doubt, will be his chief priest."

"It is only what I deserve," said Ka-Aper, giving her a mocking little bow.

"My nephew, however he might irk me with his warlike ways, does not deserve to end up as a puppet king," said Hatshepsut. "I have every intention of making Thutmose Pharaoh—when he is ready. He is young yet, and inexperienced."

"Young, yes, and full of vigor. Many are loyal to him, your Majesty," said Ka-Aper. "They believe he should be wearing the double crown. He may be inexperienced, but so is every king. It is experience he can only gain from the doing. You have carefully kept him from getting any, tucked away as he has been, under my schooling."

"A mistake, I now realize," said Hatshepsut. "I will no longer allow you to influence him."

"How? Will you remove me from office? said Ka-Aper. "Prince Thutmose would never agree to it."

"He has no say in it," said Hatshepsut.

"I think you will find that he does," said Ka-Aper. "He has had enough of your many suspected conspiracies. He will not believe you."

"Then I will have you arrested as a tomb robber,"

said Hatshepsut.

Ka-Aper laughed. "A tomb robber! No one will believe that. Whatever this child has to say, her death will silence it."

"She will not die!" said Neferhotep.

"We shall see," said Ka-Aper. "Besides, you have no other proof that I was with Seneb."

"I will find proof," said Hatshepsut. "Somehow."

Ka-Aper laughed at the Pharaoh's look of frustration.

"I had some proof," said Jennifer. "I had some beads."

"Beads?" said Hatshepsut.

"I found them on the stairs of that warehouse," said Jennifer. "I thought they might be from someone's tomb."

"Let me see them," said Hatshepsut.

Jennifer hung her head. "I can't. I lost them. In the hallway."

Ka-Aper, who had tensed briefly, relaxed again.

Grandma Jo reached into her black bag. "You mean these beads?" she asked, holding the twist of wire with its blue and gold beads in her palm. "They were in my bag. I couldn't figure out where they'd come from."

"You must have picked them up after I bumped into

you in the hall," said Jennifer, taking the beads from her and handing them to Hatshepsut.

"Hm. I believe I have seen something like these before," she said. She glanced at Ka-Aper, then rose gracefully. He struggled in the grasp of the soldiers as she approached him. When she reached him, she stared into his eyes. Then her hand darted out, quick as a snake, to fling the head of Ka-Aper's leopard skin over his shoulder. The necklace that had been hidden beneath it was composed of the same blue and gold beads. Some of them were missing.

"Ah," said Neferhotep, on a long-drawn out sigh.

Ka-Aper lowered his chin. "The old woman could have found them anywhere. In the palace corridor, for example."

"There are more gaps in your necklace," said Hatshepsut, scanning the rows of beads. "Perhaps we may find more evidence, back where you lost these."

"You left a trail," hissed Seneb.

"Quiet," said Ka-Aper, glaring at him. He turned to Hatshepsut. "Do you truly think this will convict me?"

"It will cast doubt," said Hatshepsut. "My nephew,

Thutmose, will not care to be seen consorting with criminals."

Ka-Aper shook his head. "He will not believe it. It is not enough."

Hatshepsut's fist clenched around the beads.

"What about Parahotep's map?" asked Jennifer. "He said he had it."

"Of course!" said Neferhotep, snapping his fingers. "When I looked for it in my quarters, it was gone."

"We will have his rooms searched," said Hatshepsut.

"No," said Neferhotep. "Something like that, he would keep on his person." He approached Ka-Aper and untied the small leather pouch that hung at Ka-Aper's waist. Neferhotep kept his gaze locked on Ka-Aper's as he dug around in it. He pulled his fist out around something and handed it to the Pharaoh.

It was a tightly-rolled scrap of papyrus. With her lips pressed into a thin line, she shook it out and looked at it.

"Together, this, and the pieces of your necklace are enough to condemn you as a tomb robber," she said to Ka-Aper.

"But not as a murderer," Ka-Aper said lightly.

"True," said Hatshepsut.

"Perhaps this will help," said Bibi. He reached into Seneb's leather pouch and brought out a small round alabaster vessel. "I felt it earlier, when the guards brought him to me." He handed the vessel to Neferhotep.

Neferhotep wiggled the stopper loose and sniffed at the contents. "Poison," he said to the Pharaoh.

Seneb's gaze skittered from Ka-Aper to the Pharaoh. "I was supposed to put that in your food, M-Majesty. But you didn't eat anything at the feast!"

"Quiet, fool!" said Ka-Aper.

"That is enough proof for me," said Hatshepsut.

"I demand a trial!" said Ka-Aper.

"Where you would no doubt seduce any judges to your side," said Hatshepsut. "No."

The Pharaoh stepped back. Slowly and deliberately, she crossed her arms diagonally over her chest, her palms flat against the opposite shoulders. "Witness this, all who are within the sound of my voice. I hereby pronounce judgment upon these traitors to the Double Crown. As I am Pharaoh, I am also High Priestess of Amon-Ra. Ka-Aper and Seneb, by spoken word and physical evidence, you are hereby known to be treason-ous. I strip you of your office, and sentence you to ex-ile in the Western Desert. May the gods have mercy on you." She lowered her arms.

Ka-Aper stood still, his face blank. Then it twisted into a mask of hatred. Jennifer shuddered. He didn't even look human anymore.

"Exile!" he spat.

"You deserve worse," Neferhotep growled.

"My reign is built upon peace," Hatshepsut remind-ed him. "I will not have bloodshed."

"You are weak," said Ka-Aper.

"Oh?" said Hatshepsut. "You will have no food, no water, no way to return. The desert will be your executioner."

Seneb sagged in Bibi's grip. Neferhotep put his hands behind his back and watched Ka-Aper. His lips moved soundlessly.

Ka-Aper glanced at Seneb in disgust, then raked Neferhotep with his gaze. "Very well," he said. "Exile it is. But do you think that if you kill my body, the forces arrayed against you will stop? Those who agree with me—and there are many!—will continue my work. You will not catch them all. They believe that you have stolen the throne from its rightful ruler, and your blasphemy will be repaid in the coin of destruction."

"Destruction?" said Hatshepsut.

"After your death, they will erase the memory of the woman who dared to be King," said Ka-Aper. His voice was like a hammer, pounding on the Pharaoh. "There will be none to stop them."

"My nephew…," Hatshepsut began.

"Your nephew will agree with them," said Ka-Aper. "He has been denied for too long."

"I will deal with him when the time comes," said Hatshepsut. She turned away from Ka-Aper and Seneb and reseated herself on her chair. "Take them away!"

The two guards yanked on Ka-Aper's arms, pulling him back from Hatshepsut and the others. He briefly struggled again, then finally gave up and walked with them, his head held high. As he passed Jennifer, he gave her an odd little smile. The two guards marched him out of the room between them. Bibi followed, dragging Seneb, who sobbed uncontrollably.

Jennifer took a deep breath in the sudden silence.

"They're gone, your Majesty," said Neferhotep. "Ka-Aper won't trouble you anymore."

"Oh, I expect he will trouble me for some time," said Hatshepsut. "So will his followers."

"We will find them and defeat them," said Neferhotep, his fists by his sides. "I promise it."

"Faithful one," said Hatshepsut. "I rely on friends like you." She looked at Jennifer. "And you, child. Thank you for all your help. Be assured, I will reward you for your efforts."

Jennifer shrugged. "You don't need to."

"I have something for you," said Neferhotep. "I found this in Ka-Aper's pouch." He opened his hand and held it in front of Jennifer. The scarab amulet lay in his palm.

"Oh!" said Jennifer, reaching for it. Neferhotep jerked his hand back a little, then held it out again, his gaze steady on hers. Jennifer picked it up by the thong and slipped it over her head. It thumped reassuringly against her chest, nestling amongst the folds of her dress. "Thank you."

Neferhotep frowned briefly, then nodded and stepped back. He let out a breath.

"All is well," he said.

The sound of running feet, slapping the floor of the corridor outside Hatshepsut's room, interrupted him. One of the guards who had escorted Ka-Aper ran into the room. His nose was bleeding.

"Your Majesty!" he gasped out. "Ka-Aper has escaped!"

"How?" barked Neferhotep.

"Our fault," the guard said miserably. "He was going so quietly. He wiggled out of our hold somehow and knocked our heads together. Sent us both reeling."

"Where did he go?" asked Neferhotep.

The guard shook his head. "He ran away—incredibly fast! Like the wind. We think he is still somewhere in the palace."

"What about Seneb?" asked Hatshepsut.

"We still have him. Bibi thrust him at us and went after Ka-Aper."

"He must not escape," said Hatshepsut. "Call out as many as you can and search the palace."

The guard nodded and dashed off the way he had come.

"I'm sure you'll find him," said Grandma Jo.

"He is found," a voice growled from the door to the courtyard. Ka-Aper sprinted into the room, heading for the Pharaoh. A knife glinted in his hand.

"No!" said Jennifer, diving between him and Hatshepsut.

He grinned and before anyone could stop him, he had grabbed Jennifer around the neck, from behind. He held her up against his chest and pressed the knife to her throat. Jennifer grabbed his arm, but he held her fast.

"That was foolish," he said. "No one move. Or she will die."

"What do you want?" asked Hatshepsut.

Ka-Aper laughed wildly. "Want? You know what I want."

"You may not have it. I am still Pharaoh," said Hatshepsut.

"Then say your farewells to this child," said Ka-Aper. They stared at each other.

"Wait," said Hatshepsut, rising. Ka-Aper twisted to keep her in view. All eyes followed her as she walked regally to where the Double Crown sat on the cupboard. She picked it up and held it out. "Is this what you desire?"

Bibi edged sideways.

Ka-Aper shifted his grip on Jennifer, eyeing the Crown. "For Thutmose, of course," he said.

"Of course," said Hatshepsut, walking around him with the Crown on her palms. He turned with her. "Very well."

"No!" said Neferhotep. "You…you mustn't."

"What choice do I have?" asked Hatshepsut. "One does what one must. Even if it is not popular. Release the child, and I will give it to you."

"Oh, no," said Ka-Aper. "I intend to keep a good hold on this hostage. Give me the Crown and then perhaps I will release her."

Bibi had silently worked his way behind Ka-Aper. Jennifer reached up and tugged on Ka-Aper's arm, trying to pull the knife away.

"Too bad you are not strong enough to defeat me, child," Ka-Aper purred in her ear. "I will have your life, sooner or later."

"No, you shall not." One of Bibi's arms snaked around Ka-Aper's and yanked the knife away from

Jennifer's throat. His other arm clamped around Ka-Aper's throat.

Jennifer twisted out of Ka-Aper's hands, spinning to face him. The amulet flew up and tapped him on the arm. He hissed in pain and jerked back from it. Puzzled, she frowned.

Neferhotep started forward, his eyes narrowing. His gaze darted from Ka-Aper to Jennifer and back again.

Ka-Aper flailed in Bibi's strong grasp but couldn't break it. His face purpled, his neck squeezed by Bibi's other arm.

"May I kill him, your Majesty?" said Bibi.

Hatshepsut considered. "He deserves it. For this and other crimes. Because of Ka-Aper, Bibi's daughter suffered the same fate that you almost did," she said to Jennifer. "To my shame, I was unable to stop him then. Bibi blinded himself so he would not have to see his daughter's body. His wife killed herself because of it."

Bibi's hand tightened.

"Yes," said Hatshepsut. "Do it, Bibi."

"No!" said Neferhotep.

"Why not?" Hatshepsut asked.

"Your Majesty, killing this man would serve no purpose," said Neferhotep.

"What do you mean? You were willing to let him go into exile," said Hatshepsut, gently replacing the Double Crown on top of the cupboard, "where the desert itself would certainly have done it for us."

"I…that was earlier."

"So?"

"Your Majesty, I know you do not believe in demons," said Neferhotep.

"With good reason," said Hatshepsut, glancing at Bibi.

"I believe there is one here," said Neferhotep.

"This child? Surely not."

"No," said Neferhotep.

"You think it's him, don't you," said Jennifer, looking at Ka-Aper. "He isn't afraid to go out at night."

Ka-Aper sneered.

"Yes. I think that Ka-Aper has been possessed," said Neferhotep.

Hatshepsut's eyebrows rose. "Neferhotep . . ."

"When you proclaimed yourself Pharaoh, he was one of your supporters," said Neferhotep. "I remember him as a good man, an honest one. He has changed since then."

"True. But all men are human, and he was in a position to be tempted," said Hatshepsut.

"You liked and admired him," said Neferhotep. "Did you think he was the kind of man to stoop as low as tomb robbing?"

Hatshepsut looked long at Ka-Aper, who was struggling for breath in Bibi's tight hold. "No," she said. "I did not. But Neferhotep…a demon? How can you prove it?"

"The amulet!" said Jennifer.

"Yes," said Neferhotep.

Jennifer looked down at the scarab clutched in her hand. Although he had tried to get it away from her several times, Ka-Aper had never actually touched it. Ka-Aper had only inspected the amulet by holding it by the thong. A brief encounter with it had hurt him. What would happen if she held it against him for a longer time?

She looked at Neferhotep, who nodded.

"I can't," she said. "He's been awful, but I don't want to hurt him."

"If I am right," said Neferhotep, "it will help him. Please, Dje-Nefer."

Jennifer swallowed. "All right."

She lifted the thong over her head and walked towards Ka-Aper, holding the amulet out in front of her. He watched it, his eyes going wide as she reached to touch him with it.

Ka-Aper's free arm snapped up and knocked the amulet out of Jennifer's grasp. Grandma Jo gasped as it flew upwards, spinning in the light from the lamps. It paused at the top of the arc, then began its descent to the hard stone below, where it would surely shatter. Without the amulet, there would be no way they could get home!

"No!" Jennifer choked out. She dived for it, sliding on the tiles with her hand outstretched. The amulet smacked into it. She closed her fingers around the smooth stone and gripped it tight.

"Yes!" said Grandma Jo, one arm pumping the air. "Good catch, shortstop!"

Neferhotep gave her an odd look, then kneeled to wrap his arms around Ka-Aper's legs. Bibi had pinned his arms. Jennifer rose and turned to face Ka-Aper again.

Wary of him, Jennifer reached out slowly, then pressed the amulet to the skin over his heart. Ka-Aper screeched, his tone rising upward to a high-pitched whine that she felt in her teeth and her bones.

A sudden whirlwind whipped at the hair of all those within. Grains of sand swirled upwards, spiraling around them, battering their skin. Jennifer couldn't breathe as the air was sucked away from her body by the storm.

Ka-Aper's body arched backwards, bending him almost in two. From his chest, a translucent black cloud rose and floated to the ceiling. Two glowing red eyes in the center of the cloud glared at them for a moment. Then it shrieked and shot out through the door to the courtyard. A foul stench of rotten garbage lingered.

The whirlwind came to a whispering stop. Ka-Aper closed his eyes and his body collapsed, seeming to shrink in on itself. As they watched, wrinkles deepened on his face, aging him years in front of them. He took a deep, shuddering breath. A moment later, his eyes fluttered open.

"Wh—where am I?" he said in a hoarse, weak voice.

Bibi let go of his arms. Ka-Aper's gaze took in all those around him, staring. Hatshepsut's hands were at her lips. "Your Majesty?"

"Ka-Aper?" she said.

"Yes…at least, I think so," he said. He blinked several times, then let his head fall forward. "Oh, dear. What has happened?"

"You were possessed by a demon," Neferhotep said softly. He reached under Ka-Aper's shoulders to help him sit up.

"A demon! Oh, my," said Ka-Aper. "I seem to remember…" He tried to rise, but his legs wouldn't hold him. He looked up at Hatshepsut. "I hope I didn't do anything too awful."

She smiled down at him. "I am glad to see you back, my old friend."

Hatshepsut sagged into her chair as Bibi led the old man away. Exhausted, Jennifer sank to the bench beside Grandma Jo. For a few moments, they sat in silence, their breathing settling into a quiet rhythm. Then Hatshepsut turned and gave Neferhotep a weary smile.

"I suppose I must believe in demons, now," she said.

"I'm just glad it was defeated," he said.

"Yes." She glanced at Jennifer. "We should reassure your family that you are well. Your uncle will know where to find them."

Neferhotep left but was back in moments with Meryt-Re, Ramose, Mentmose, and surprisingly, Tetisheri and her parents, Satyah and Hekhanakhte. They walked in, then stopped, startled, when they saw the Pharaoh. All of them immediately kneeled. Hatshepsut gestured for them to rise and come closer.

"Here is your daughter," she said. "Safe and sound."

Tetisheri ran to Jennifer and swept her into a hug. "Are you all right, Dje-Nefer? When that horrible man said you were a demon, I was so scared. And so glad

241

when you ran away from him. Ra, but he was angry!"

"You didn't think I was possessed by a demon?" asked Jennifer, gently disentangling herself from Tetisheri's arms.

"Of course not!" said Tetisheri. "How could you be? I know you. And besides, Miw rubbed up against you, remember? A cat wouldn't do that if she didn't know it was safe."

Meryt-Re and Ramose approached slowly. Jennifer stood and Meryt-Re peered into her eyes. "Dje-Nefer?"

"Don't worry, Meryt-Re, she is not a demon," said Neferhotep. "She has not been possessed by a Walker of the Night."

"Are you sure?" asked Ramose.

"The amulet is the proof. She can bear its touch, as Ka-Aper was unable to do."

Meryt-Re sighed and stood straighter. "I was wrong to have doubted you, Dje-Nefer."

Ramose smiled at her. "I, also. Can you forgive us, my daughter?"

Jennifer nodded. "Sure."

"Neferhotep, I wish you hadn't made us worry so," said Ramose.

"I was afraid for her. And for you." Neferhotep paused. "However, there is something you should know."

"What now?" said Ramose.

"This girl is not a demon. But she is not your daughter."

Jennifer froze.

"What do you mean?" said Meryt-Re.

"Yes, Neferhotep," said Hatshepsut. "Please explain."

"I wish I could. There are too many things unexplained, your Majesty," said Neferhotep. "I know my niece well, and I know she would never get lost in this city. There were other indicators. Meryt-Re, had you not noticed your daughter was acting strange?"

"I was not worried at first," said Meryt-Re, spreading her hands wide, "but I began to be, especially when I recalled your mention of demons…"

"No." Neferhotep paced closer to Jennifer. He put his hands on her shoulders and looked her in the eyes. "No, not a demon, I know. What are you, child?" he asked softly.

Jennifer swallowed and looked at Grandma Jo. "Should we tell them?"

"Mutemwija?" said Meryt-Re. "What are you doing here?"

"I'm not really Mutemwija. My name is Josephine."

"Mine is Jennifer. I…we…are time travelers," said Jennifer.

Hatshepsut's eyebrows rose.

"Time travelers!" Ramose burst out laughing. "You are joking, are you not?"

"It's the truth," said Grandma Jo.

"Time travelers," Neferhotep said slowly, drawing out each syllable. Then he grinned, more widely than she had ever seen him smile. "Travelers through time! This is wonderful!"

Jennifer couldn't help smiling back. Of course he would believe her. At least she'd made one person happy. "I woke up here on the morning of the day we had dinner with Ka-Aper."

"Ridiculous," harrumphed Tetisheri's father, coming forward. "Majesty…"

Satyah looked skeptical too. "The child is telling tales."

"No, I don't think so," said Neferhotep.

Hekhanakhte started to open his mouth, then stiffened and swayed for a moment. He braced himself against the wall, giving Jennifer a penetrating stare. Puzzled, she turned away from him.

"But she looks like Dje-Nefer," said Meryt-Re. "I would swear this is my daughter."

"We exchanged bodies, I think," said Jennifer. "Dje-Nefer is in my body, in my time."

"Mutemwija, poor lady, is in mine," said Grandma Jo. "We look similar, however. I was shocked to see something like my own reflection in a mirror."

"But how can this be?" asked Meryt-Re. "How can someone be in another's body?"

"It may have something to do with their ka," Neferhotep mused.

"Their life forces?" asked Ramose.

"Yes," said Neferhotep, in a detached, almost scientific voice. "Or possibly the akh, the personality. But not the ba. That part is created after death, and you are not dead. Are you?"

"I don't think so," said Jennifer. "Although sometimes I think I'm dreaming."

245

Grandma Jo chuckled. "Me, too."

"Dreaming...," said Neferhotep. "I remember you mentioned you had dreamed of Amon-Ra that morning. Dreams are omens."

"Perhaps...perhaps your holy father had something to do with this, your Majesty," said Hekhanakhte. Satyah glanced at him, frowning.

"Amon-Ra?" asked Hatshepsut. "But why?"

Neferhotep shrugged. "Has not this child done you a great service?"

"Certainly."

"Maybe he sent her," said Neferhotep. "To help you."

Hatshepsut leaned back in her chair and eyed Jennifer. "It could be so."

"But...how?" said Meryt-Re.

Neferhotep turned to Jennifer. "Yes, exactly. How did you come to be here?"

Jennifer lifted her amulet. "It was this."

"The amulet of Amon-Ra!" said Neferhotep. "It is his sacred symbol."

"Wait," said Ramose, shaking his head. "I don't understand. You said you woke up here yesterday morning."

Jennifer nodded slowly. Had she only been here for two days? It seemed longer.

"But that means I gave you the amulet after you had, um, traveled through time," said Ramose. "How could that be?"

"The traveling happened in the future, in my time," she said. "I opened the amulet when I received it then."

"That was—or will be—thousands of years from now," said Grandma Jo.

Ramose flashed a white grin. "My work has lasted that long?"

"Yours, and the work of many others," Grandma Jo assured him. "We have hundreds of thousands of pieces still from this time period."

"Pieces?" said Hatshepsut. "Then this land of ours is no longer intact, in your world?"

"Oh, no," said Grandma Jo. "It's still there. But in the grand scheme of things, we do not have much left of your civilization. A lot of it has been destroyed."

"Even the pyramids?" asked Hekhanakhte.

"No, they are still there," said Grandma Jo. "They are considered one of the wonders of our modern world.

And we have other relics—statues, tomb paintings, pots and jars. Even some food and plants."

"Food and plants? They are still recognizable, after all those years?" asked Neferhotep.

"Some. The mummified or petrified ones. Not everything survived."

"Most of the temples are in ruins," said Jennifer.

"Ruins!" said Mentmose. "But they are made of stone. How could they be in ruins?"

"Time is not kind to the works of man," said Grandma Jo. "Nor is war or the movements of the earth. There have been earthquakes, among other things, over the last thirty-five hundred years. Some of your artifacts are reduced to rubble."

"Thirty-five hundred years!" said Neferhotep. "So long a time…"

"It is good to know that we are still remembered," said Hekhanakhte.

"Sure," said Jennifer. "We even study your civilization in school."

"School? You go to school?" asked Mentmose. "Why would you go to school? You are a girl, aren't you?"

248

"Of course she is," said Tetisheri. "Don't be silly. She knows all about being a girl."

"Everyone goes to school in my time," said Jennifer.

"I must admit, I feel very odd being the topic of a history discussion," said Hatshepsut.

"Oh, you're famous," Jennifer assured her. "The female Pharaoh!"

"I hope my mortuary temple of Djeser-Djeseru still remains," said Hatshepsut.

"It was destroyed," said Jennifer. "But it's being restored."

"Destroyed?" said Neferhotep. "How could anyone damage such a beautiful thing? It is one of the loveliest in all of Kemet."

"It's not just your temple," said Jennifer. "Everything. Your statues, your tomb paintings, your cartouches, your name. All gone."

"Gone?" said Meryt-Re, with a gasp.

"But then…how…?" said Neferhotep. "How do you know she exists? Existed?"

"A few things survived," said Jennifer. "Whoever did it didn't destroy your obelisks, just plastered them over.

We found them, and other items, fairly recently."

"Then I am not completely forgotten," said Hatshepsut.

"No," said Jennifer. "Although you were for centuries. We didn't know even your name until just recently."

"Ka-Aper predicted this," said Hatshepsut. "Who is it that carries out the destruction?"

"No one knows who did it," said Jennifer. "Some people think it was done by Thutmose, after he becomes Pharaoh."

"You are saying he will succeed me," said Hatshepsut.

"Yes, and soon," said Jennifer. "You did say you had already reigned for twenty years, didn't you?"

"Yes," said Hatshepsut. "It has been that long."

"Our archeologists have decided you were on the throne for about twenty to twenty-two years."

"So my nephew gets his revenge."

"We don't know for sure that it was Thutmose," Jennifer reminded her.

"It seems most likely," said Hatshepsut. "I know he

is…disaffected."

"He wants to be King," said Neferhotep.

"He should be," said Tetisheri. "He's been waiting long enough."

"Teti!" said Satyah.

"Well, it's true," said Tetisheri. "You even said so."

"Pardon my daughter," said Satyah, with a little gasp. "She doesn't know what she's saying."

Hekhanakhte nodded, sweating a little.

Hatshepsut chuckled. "I think she does." She rose and took a step towards Jennifer and Tetisheri.

"Your majesty," said Satyah, "Please. She is young…"

Tetisheri fumbled for Jennifer's hand. Jennifer automatically held it and gave it a squeeze.

"So you think Thutmose should be on the throne?" she asked Tetisheri.

Tetisheri gulped, then nodded. Hatshepsut's face was expressionless, but Jennifer thought she saw a brief smile soften it.

Satyah dropped to the tiled floor, kneeling. "Your Majesty…Pharaoh…please don't hurt my daughter."

Hatshepsut frowned at her. "I would not hurt a child."

"But your soldiers…"

"As has been pointed out to me, my soldiers are acting without my orders," said Hatshepsut. "I think perhaps they are no longer my soldiers. In any case, I would not let them harm her. In fact, I salute her honesty. I value those who speak their minds to me and do not pretend one thing and yet say another." Hatshepsut turned her attention once more to Tetisheri. "Child, you may be right. I will think on it. You were very brave to tell me."

Mentmose looked at Tetisheri, a thoughtful expression on his face.

Hekhanakhte helped Satyah to rise from the floor.

Meryt-Re stepped forward. "Pharaoh, what can we do to return my daughter to me?"

"In no way do I know how this situation could come to be," said Hatshepsut. "Perhaps you should ask Neferhotep that question."

"You said the amulet sent you here?" Neferhotep asked Jennifer.

"Actually, it was the dust inside it," said Jennifer.

"Dust? What kind of dust?" asked Neferhotep.

"I don't know," said Jennifer, shaking her head. "It

was just dust. It smelled like the stuff you have in those storage jars that we found when we were hiding."

"Myrrh?" said Neferhotep. "That's easily provided. But the dust could be anything."

"I thought the dust in the amulet would send me back the first time I opened it here," said Jennifer. "But it was empty."

"Neferhotep was going to fill it," said Ramose.

Jennifer slid her fingernail into the hairline crack around the edge. "There's nothing in there now..." She stopped, as the amulet's top flipped up. Inside, there was a small mound of ground up herbs. "Where did this come from?"

"I put it in there," said Neferhotep. "Earlier today, I made up a mixture of herbs that are recommended for the exorcism of demons, and said a spell over it—just in case. After I took the amulet from Ka-Aper, I put the mixture in it."

Jennifer raised her eyebrows.

"It worked on Ka-Aper," said Neferhotep. "You know what happened to him."

"What did happen to him?" asked Ramose.

Hatshepsut let out a tired sigh. "It seems my priest had been possessed for years. The demon has been vanquished. I fear that my old friend Ka-Aper will never be the same again, however. Bibi is taking care of him right now."

"Some of the other priests told me Ka-Aper had been meddling with old, forbidden subjects," said Neferhotep. "Potions, spells…Perhaps he inadvertently called a demon to him. In any case, the demon's reaction to the amulet told me much. But because you could wear it without fear, I knew you weren't a demon."

"I told you so," said Tetisheri.

"You were right," said Neferhotep, nodding at her. "So, now we need to work on how to send you home."

"I suppose so," said Jennifer. She slowly closed the lid of her amulet.

"Must they leave us so soon?" asked Tetisheri.

"We have to," said Jennifer. She looked at Meryt-Re, who was missing a daughter. "Although I wish I could stay a little longer."

"I don't want you to go. Not yet," said Tetisheri. "I don't care who you are. I like you."

"Thank you," said Jennifer, giving her a warm smile.

"Are boys the same in your time?" asked Tetisheri.

"Well," said Jennifer, glancing at Mentmose. She realized she didn't really know. Maybe she should have paid more attention to Kelly and Ashley!

"Teti," said Satyah. "I don't think you should talk to this...person."

"Why not? She's not going to hurt me," said Tetisheri. She turned a blazing smile on Jennifer. "Are you?"

"No," said Jennifer. "Of course not."

"Oh, Tetisheri," said Satyah. "You trust so easily. Some day..."

"She was always a loyal girl, Satyah," said Meryt-Re.

"To everyone," said Mentmose. He blushed and smiled at Tetisheri. "Even me."

Tetisheri beamed at him.

"We should speak of that," said Satyah. "Soon."

"Mother?" said Tetisheri.

"Things have changed since you were betrothed," said Satyah.

"It is only you who have changed, Satyah," Meryt-Re said quietly.

"I would be happy to have Mentmose as a son-in-law,"

said Hekhanakhte. Satyah whipped her head around to stare at him.

"Things may change yet again," said Hatshepsut. "Change is, as we have seen, inevitable. We would do well to remember that."

"Of course, your Majesty," said Meryt-Re.

"Yes, Pharaoh," said Satyah, bowing.

"Speaking of change, after we have discovered how to send these people where they want to be, Ramose, I would like to discuss a royal commission with you. Apparently, it is time I prepared myself for my death."

Tetisheri gasped. "Your death?"

"It comes to us all, child," said Hatshepsut, gently. "Even to countries, it seems. We cannot avoid it, but we can make provision for it, before we all crumble to dust." She turned to Jennifer. "Was my mummy also destroyed, along with everything else?"

"We thought it might have been," said Jennifer. "But it was just hidden."

"Hidden?"

"As a precaution, probably. Your mummy was just recently identified."

"Are they sure?"

"Beyond a doubt," said Jennifer. "They found a box with your cartouche on it, which held a tooth you had lost."

Hatshepsut put a hand on her cheek. "A tooth?"

"It was matched to your mummy. Then there was the DNA evidence…"

"The what?" asked Neferhotep.

"Never mind, Neferhotep. Thank you, Dje-, I mean, Jennifer. It is good indeed to know that my existence in the afterlife is assured. At least I have not crumbled away to dust," said Hatshepsut.

"Dust…" said Jennifer. She peered at her amulet. "Grandma, you don't suppose this was filled with… mummy dust?"

"No, no. I feel sure Daoud wouldn't have allowed that. He had a deep reverence for his country and its history. If he did put the dust in there, it would not have been from a mummy. Though some people did grind them up, in Victorian times."

"Ra!" said Mentmose. "You grind up our mummies?"

"Oh, not anymore," Grandma Jo assured him. "No

one is allowed to do that. When we find your tombs, we put the items in a museum."

"Museum?" said Neferhotep.

"It's a kind of place where all sorts of people can come to view ancient artifacts," said Jennifer. "Ours has a traveling exhibition of stuff from your country right now."

"Including a most fascinating fragment of a tomb painting," said Grandma Jo. She winked at Jennifer.

"Amazing," said Neferhotep. "Is that where you found the amulet?"

"No. Well, sort of. The curator gave it to me. Grandma, do you think Daoud knew what would happen when I opened it?" she asked. "Do you think he put the dust in the amulet?"

"I don't know. Maybe."

"If he did, then we have no hope of going home," said Jennifer. "He's not here."

"Maybe it was something from our time that did it," said Tetisheri. "Something that had been in there for, oh, centuries."

"Like what?" said Jennifer. "After that long, anything

we put in it would be…dust." Her eyes went wide. "Dust! These herbs…in my time, they would be dust."

Tetisheri clapped her hands over her mouth.

"These plants were meant for banishing a demon," warned Neferhotep. "They worked for that. Ka-Aper is free; the demon is gone from us. But this…"

"Maybe they could 'banish' us, too," said Jennifer.

"I don't know any spells for that," Neferhotep began. Meryt-Re put her hand on his arm.

"Try," she said.

"I don't know what would happen," said Neferhotep. "It might need something else to make it work that way. I'm sorry. I don't know what that would be."

"Myrrh!" said Jennifer.

"Of course," Neferhotep said softly. "Myrrh is one of the items that we use to anoint our mummies, to assist them in their travel to the next world."

Hatshepsut rose and walked to the little cupboard which held the Double Crown, then opened the painted door and reached inside, bringing out a small glass bottle. She held it carefully as she returned, then handed it to Neferhotep. He held it up to the light. Golden liquid moved sluggishly within.

"Myrrh," he said. He removed the stopper and sniffed. "The finest kind, too."

"Naturally," said Hatshepsut, one side of her mouth lifting.

Neferhotep turned to Jennifer and held out his hand. "May I?" he asked.

Jennifer lifted the amulet over her head and gave it to him. He opened it, then poured several drops of the fragrant incense into the mixture of herbs. Shutting the amulet firmly, he gave it a vigorous shake. Finally, he pressed the amulet to his forehead and closed his eyes, then muttered some words.

"There," he said, re-opening his eyes. "Now it is up to you."

Tetisheri, off to the side with her parents, took in a breath like a sob. Hekhanakhte hugged her around the shoulders, then shook his head as if trying to clear it. He swayed a little, then smiled down at his daughter.

Jennifer took the amulet from Neferhotep and walked to Grandma Jo's bench. Sitting beside her, Jennifer lay the amulet flat on her palm and prepared to open it.

"Are you ready?" she asked.

"Are you?" Grandma Jo countered.

Jennifer paused. She didn't really want to go. But she knew she had to. She scanned the room, gazing at the family and friends she had known for so short a time.

Mentmose had moved close to Tetisheri and was holding her hand. Satyah and Hekhanakhte, who stood off to one side, didn't seem to notice. Neferhotep was watching Jennifer and Grandma Jo closely and gave them an encouraging nod. Ramose had his arm around Meryt-Re, whose fists were pressed tightly against her chest. She held her breath, waiting. Jennifer nodded. Waiting for Dje-Nefer to return.

"Stop," said Meryt-Re, lifting Ramose's arm away from her. She approached Jennifer, then enveloped her in a hug. "Though I want my daughter back, I will be sorry to see you go. Farewell."

Jennifer swallowed and brushed at her eyes. "Thank you."

Last of all, Jennifer looked at Hatshepsut, the female Pharaoh. "If this works, I guess this is goodbye," she said.

"I will not forget you…Jennifer," said the Pharaoh.

"I won't forget you, either," said Jennifer.

"Then I am content," said Hatshepsut.

Jennifer looked at Grandma Jo and flipped open the amulet. "Let's go."

Both of them sniffed, hard. At first, nothing happened. Jennifer sighed, and her breath stirred the sticky mixture. The smell of the sharp myrrh was tinted with the scent of the other ingredients.

Her eyesight blurred. Then the world tilted and suddenly she was surrounded by the familiar, gold-shot darkness. For a moment, she thought she saw a ghostly outline of a man wearing a tall, white, split headdress.

And then, nothing.

Jennifer pushed past some of the other kids from Mrs. Goodwin's class, deftly avoiding Tyler's outstretched foot, and pulled Hannah over to the case containing the cosmetic pots.

"This is what I was talking about," she said.

Hannah peered at them, then raised her perfectly plucked eyebrows. "So?"

"They're for make-up," said Jennifer. "See that little stick? They dipped it in kohl and drew lines around their eyes with it."

"Eyeliner?" said Hannah. "Huh."

A small glass bottle, with thick white wavy lines, just like the one Hatshepsut had used for myrrh, stood next to the clay pots.

"And that one was for perfume," said Jennifer. "They used a lot of scents."

"Cool," said Hannah, bending to get a closer look. "I wonder where I could get some."

"They might sell replicas in the gift shop," said Jennifer.

"Is that where you got your necklace?" asked Hannah.

Jennifer cupped the amulet, faded and chipped by time, in her hand. She had threaded it onto a leather cord so she could wear it as a pendant. "No. Someone gave it to me. A friend."

"Nice friend," said Hannah.

"You like it?"

"It's okay," Hannah said, trying to sound indifferent. She stroked the back of the scarab with one finger.

"Hey, what's up?" said Kelly as she and Ashley joined them.

Hannah shrugged, dropping her hand. "Not much."

"Did you see the mummy?" asked Ashley.

"Yes, and ew, it's gross," said Kelly.

"At least it's better than all those ceramic pots," said Ashley. "Borrrrring!"

"The tomb painting's kind of neat, though," said Kelly. "Did you see it, Jen? There's a girl on it that looks a lot like you!"

"Yeah, I saw it," said Jennifer, smiling.

"By the way, we love what you did to your hair," said Hannah.

"It took the stylist hours to do all the tiny braids,"

said Jennifer. "My grandmother paid for it." She liked the way it looked in her mirror, even though it wasn't glossy black.

Hannah fingered her long blonde hair. "Maybe I should get mine done, too."

"That would be cool," said Jennifer.

"Hey, why aren't you listening to that Egyptologist guy?" asked Kelly. "I thought you were really into this stuff. I mean, you took all those books and videos out of the library."

"I've seen it before," said Jennifer, shrugging. She looked over to where Daoud and a young, dark-skinned woman were talking about the ushabtis to Mrs. Goodwin and some of the kids. "Grandma Jo and I got a personal tour a couple of weeks ago."

"Hey, has your grandmother talked your mom and dad into letting you go with her when she goes to Egypt next year?" asked Kelly.

"She's working on them," said Jennifer, grinning. "So am I."

They were reluctant, but Jennifer had been mentioning the educational benefits. A lot. She and Grandma Jo were pretty sure her parents were about to cave in.

"Do you want to get together at my house after school so we can work on our Egyptian house project?" asked Kelly. Hannah rolled her eyes.

"Okay," said Ashley. "I'll ask my mom if we can use some of her dollhouse modeling clay. She showed me how to make tiles with it a couple of weeks ago."

"You into that?" asked Hannah. "It sounds boring."

Ashley shrugged. "It's fun. We made pots and bowls with it, too. I'll show you."

"Oh, all right," said Hannah.

"Okay," said Jennifer. "We could do it today, but not tomorrow. I have a ball game."

"Can I come?" asked Hannah. "Your coach is cute."

"Sure. I'll even introduce you," said Jennifer, with a wiggle of her eyebrows. Hannah giggled.

Mrs. Goodwin called out to the class. Daoud and the young woman were taking them to the other room now. Jennifer, Ashley, Kelly and Hannah tagged along at the end of the file. At the door, Jennifer paused and looked over her shoulder at the mummy and its tomb painting. She let the others get ahead of her, then slipped back.

Somebody had moved things around a bit since her last visit. There was a bench in front of the painting now. Jennifer sat on it and held her amulet.

"Hi, Dje-Nefer," she said softly to the girl in the painting. "I wonder how your life went after I left. I hope you had a good one."

"Jennifer?"

Startled, Jennifer jerked her attention away from the tomb fragment. Daoud was standing beside the bench. "May I sit?"

"Sure," said Jennifer. "I thought you were giving a tour to my class."

"My assistant, Rasha, is doing that. She is very knowledgeable about the later time periods," said Daoud. "So I can talk with you."

He and Jennifer looked at the tomb painting. It really was a very good likeness.

Jennifer cleared her throat. "Daoud? You knew what was going to happen when I opened the amulet, didn't you?"

Daoud was silent for a moment. Then he sighed. "Yes. I knew."

Jennifer waited. Daoud glanced at her and gave her a tired smile. The lines in his aged face seemed deeper than before.

"As you say in English, it is a long story," said Daoud. "It began, as you know, several thousand years ago."

"About thirty-five hundred," said Jennifer. "During Hatshepsut's time."

"Quite so. I remember it well," said Daoud.

Jennifer nodded. "Because you were there."

"Yes." For a moment, he seemed to waver, and the image of a bare-chested man wearing a white kilt and a tall split head-dress floated in front of him. Jennifer looked from him to the statue in the corner of the room. The image winked out, revealing Daoud's old, friendly face once again.

"Amon-Ra," said Jennifer, in a satisfied tone. "It was you that I saw, when Grandma Jo and I traveled back to this time, wasn't it?"

"I am Amon-Ra," Daoud confirmed. "Much diminished, of course."

"So does that mean you're a god?"

"That is not precisely the right term. Although,

to the people of Ancient Egypt, my people must have seemed that way," he said. "There never were very many of us, and we tried to keep hidden, as much as possible. Some of us were…odd-looking."

"Neferhotep and Hatshepsut said they thought they had seen you," said Jennifer.

"I'm sure they did. Even we had to eat some time," said Daoud. He winked. "And why shouldn't we consume the good food given to us as sacrifices?"

Jennifer laughed.

"We were probably seen many times. We live a long time, unless we are killed. Long enough to be considered immortal. I myself am more than five thousand years old."

"Wow," said Jennifer. "You must have been through a lot. Wars, and other stuff."

"Sadly, many of those," he sighed. "You humans are…energetic."

"Humans? Are you…aliens?" asked Jennifer.

Daoud laughed. "Oh, no. We belong to this planet, too. We are merely older beings. Do you not have stories of creatures other than man, with supernatural powers, even in your culture?"

"Well, sure," said Jennifer. "Elves, fairies—things like that."

"Just so," said Daoud. "They probably stem from the same source. We have certain talents that you do not. Do you know of telepathy, telekinesis, that sort of thing?"

"Um, telepathy is mind-reading, isn't it?"

"Speaking mind to mind, rather. Telekinesis is moving objects only with the mind," said Daoud. "Some of us have other talents, like taking over an animal or human body."

"You mean possession! Like the demon took over Ka-Aper," said Jennifer.

"Yes. Poor man."

"And...I took over Dje-Nefer. Then...am I like you?" asked Jennifer.

Daoud shook his head. "You are human. It was I who caused you to switch bodies with her."

"You? I thought the amulet and the dust did it," said Jennifer. She looked at her amulet. The dust was long gone.

Daoud clasped his hands together. "Partially. The dust was made of certain elements that are not easily obtained today. The mixture is one that our people used as a focusing agent, to assist our powers. When humans got their hands on the recipe, they used it for other purposes."

"Like getting rid of demons?"

"Yes. They found out it had an effect on some of us. Even though the mixture was greatly weakened by age, it was still effective for me. It took a lot of effort on my part, and I am weakened with age, too. I had to rest for several days after I sent your ka through time."

"Is that one of your powers?" asked Jennifer. "Time travel, I mean?"

"Not precisely," said Daoud. "I can cause a human's personality to move to another's. It was made easier by the fact that you and Dje-Nefer were so similar."

"Why did you make us switch bodies?"

"It was the only way. I couldn't send you physically."

"Why did you send me back?"

"I knew what you had to do. What you had done, actually. In the past."

"You mean Hatshepsut? The conspiracy?"

"Exactly. I didn't know what had happened at the time, of course. I only realized what you had done after you had done it," said Daoud. "I didn't even know you were there, until the entity that had possessed the unfortunate Ka-Aper had released him."

"The demon," said Jennifer.

Daoud sighed. "No more a demon than I am a god. Just someone who had the power to take over a human consciousness. When he left Ka-Aper's body, I realized what had happened."

"How did you know? You weren't there," said Jennifer.

"I was there." He lowered his voice and intoned, "It is good to know that we are still remembered." His outline wavered again, as a faint image of Tetisheri's father faded in and out.

"Hekhanakhte!" said Jennifer. "You were him!"

"For a short time," said Daoud. "Like that other entity, I also have the ability to put my consciousness in a human body, for a short time. Or I did, once."

Jennifer tilted her head to one side. "Hatshepsut said you were her true father…"

"I admit I was much taken with her mother, Ahmose," said Daoud. "She was beautiful. I would like to think that Hatshepsut was my daughter in spirit. I admired her. But, no. I did not possess Thutmose the First. I do not feel it is ethical to meddle with another person. The few times that I did, I did not enjoy it."

"You controlled me," said Jennifer. "You made me go to Dje-Nefer's body."

Daoud ducked his head. "I know. It was necessary. You were there, so you must have gone. I had to make sure that you did."

"How did you find out?"

"When I possessed Hekhanakhte, I heard your explanation of who you were, and it was then that I realized that I, or someone like me, must have caused you to travel through time. I didn't know why, then."

"But you did later."

"I did know that the demon was becoming more powerful, and I had only just found out his plans to kill Hatshepsut. I didn't know what to do. Then you showed up. Later, I decided that I myself had sent you. I waited a very long time to give you a certain amulet. I did not know that it would be centuries. Then, a few weeks ago, a girl who looked just like Dje-Nefer came to the museum."

"Me," said Jennifer.

"You," Daoud agreed.

"Why me?" asked Jennifer. "Why not some other girl? There must have been others who looked like her."

"There were a few other girls who looked something like Dje-Nefer. It could have been one of them. Only you would have known that Hatshepsut's mummy had been found."

"Because I was born in the right time," said Jennifer.

"Yes, precisely. Also, I recognized your grandmother when she came to Egypt. She looked much like Mutemwija even when she was younger," said Daoud. "I was tempted to give the amulet to her then. But she was not the one who was supposed to have it. Afterwards, I thought that perhaps if I found her again, I might find you. So I acquired an official education and made sure that this collection of artifacts came to your city. Your grandmother had told me where she lived. I hoped she had not moved."

"Couldn't you just have used your, um, powers, to locate her? Or to come here?"

Daoud shook his head. "I am very old. I still have

some of my powers, but they are weak."

"So you gave me the amulet and waited."

"I didn't know exactly when you would go, but I hoped it would be soon."

"Why?"

"So I could apologize to you," said Daoud. "I hoped I would still be in this country when you traveled through time. I felt that neither you nor I had any choice in the matter, and that distressed me. Unlike that other entity, I honor free will."

"Why did he possess poor old Ka-Aper?" asked Jennifer.

"I don't know. Perhaps he wanted to be the power behind the throne," said Daoud. "I think he did not like the way the country was being run and thought he could remove Hatshepsut from her throne. There are always some who prefer that those around them conform in predictable ways. They don't like independent thought," said Daoud. "Hatshepsut upset the normal order of things. Also, the 'demon' stayed away from his own body for too long. It had died. I think that drove him mad."

"Who was he?"

"I don't know. His essence disappeared."

A sudden burst of clapping came from the other room, then voices rose. It sounded like Mrs. Goodwin was coming back with the rest of the class. Jennifer gave the tomb painting one last look and rose. So did Daoud.

Jennifer stroked the scarab amulet. "Was this buried with Dje-Nefer?"

"Yes."

"So how did you get it?"

"I...retrieved it at about the same time that Hatshepsut's existence was rediscovered."

"You robbed her tomb?" Jennifer grinned at Daoud.

"Please. Trained Egyptologists do not rob tombs," he said, his eyes crinkling.

"You weren't trained back then."

"Back then, most 'Egyptologists' weren't more than tomb robbers themselves."

Jennifer laughed. "I should probably give this back to you," she said, about to lift the amulet over her head. Daoud held up a hand.

"No," he said. "It is most definitely yours. After all, Ramose gave it to you."

"All right." She hadn't really wanted to part with it. "Thank you," she said, smiling. "For everything."

"Thank you," said Daoud. "You did more than you know."

Jennifer glanced at the tomb painting. "I think I might learn more about hieroglyphs, so I can read this fascinating story."

"Good idea," said Daoud. "Now that you have had some experience, do you think you will be an Egyptologist when you become an adult?"

Jennifer watched as Hannah and the others walked into the room. Hannah waved to Jennifer, then tugged Ashley and Kelly along to see the cosmetics containers. Jennifer patted her braided hair.

"I don't know," she said, grinning, "but I do know I'll be myself."

EPILOGUE

Dje-Nefer picked up her bottle of kohl. Using her new bronze mirror, she carefully painted dark lines around her eyes.

"Are you ready?" asked Meryt-Re. Her voice echoed off the newly-plastered walls of Dje-Nefer's room. They were bare yet; Dje-Nefer would have to do something about that.

They had all moved into the villa shortly after the great Nile flood had receded. It was just one of many changes since her magical experience. It was hard to believe it had happened more than a year ago.

"I'm ready," she said. She linked arms with her mother as they walked down the hall toward the atrium.

True to her word, Pharaoh Hatshepsut had given Ramose a royal commission, and even appointed him as the royal amulet-maker. Thutmose III, pleased with his work, had kept him in the position even after Hatshepsut's death.

"Is Uncle Neferhotep joining us?" asked Dje-Nefer.

"Perhaps later. He had work to do at the palace."

Neferhotep's duties had increased with his promotion. Kai was long gone and Neferhotep had taken over Ka-Aper's duties when the old fellow had retired to a country home. After all, he had been possessed by a demon.

So had Dje-Nefer, in a way. She stroked the little scarab amulet. Ramose had carved more hieroglyphs into the stone.

"I wonder if Jennifer made it back to her own time," said Dje-Nefer.

"I suppose we will never really know," said Meryt-Re. "I hope so. She deserved to, after what she did for all of us."

When they reached the great room that served as a greeting area, Mutemwija was already there. Dje-Nefer hugged the old woman. After her adventure, Dje-Nefer had sought her out in the market. Their reunion had been so noisy and joyous that the other merchants still remarked upon it. She tried to visit every day, though she had to admit, lately she'd been going for a different reason.

"Did Ti not come with you tonight?" asked Meryt-Re.

"No. A wealthy customer wanted to make a large order. I left him to do the haggling," said Mutemwija. She smiled at Dje-Nefer. "He wanted to come, though. I think it was not just to accompany me."

Dje-Nefer blushed.

Mentmose skidded into the room, earning a frown from Meryt-Re.

"Is she here yet?" he asked.

"Teti and her parents should be arriving soon," Meryt-Re assured him.

Dje-Nefer hid a smile. Mentmose had been told he didn't have to marry Tetisheri, but it seemed he had learned to appreciate his chatty wife-to-be during Dje-Nefer's absence.

Drus, one of the new servants, came trotting up. "Excuse me, ma'am. There is a traveler at the gates. A Nubian."

"It must be Bibi," said Dje-Nefer. "Uncle Nefer told me he'd be coming by. I'll go meet him."

"All right," said Meryt-Re. "But don't be long."

Dje-Nefer walked out into the wide courtyard. Halfway across, she stopped to caress the trunk of the myrrh tree which she had transplanted from the palace. Just last week, she had harvested the golden grains, then mixed them with herbs that Neferhotep had given her. The mixture was sealed in a clay pot, waiting for her to transfer it to the amulet. Neferhotep thought the appropriate time for the ritual would be at the next rising of Sepdet, the dog star, which would be soon.

A man was waiting for her at the villa's entrance, accompanied by a scrawny donkey.

"Good evening, Dje-Nefer," said Bibi, pulling off his floppy straw hat to wipe his brow.

"Hello, Bibi. I thought you would have been long gone to Nubia by now," said Dje-Nefer.

"Your uncle asked for my help making the fake mummy," said Bibi. "We used wood and straw, then wrapped it in linen."

"You did a good job," said Dje-Nefer. "I thought the finished product was very flattering."

"Neferhotep has already hidden the real Pharaoh. Only he knows where."

"I'm sure she's pleased. The funeral procession was magnificent," said Dje-Nefer.

Exactly seventy days after Hatshepsut's death, a long line of mourners and a winding trail of servants carrying furniture, food, jewelry and pots of myrrh had followed the Pharaoh's sarcophagus to her temple near the Valley of the Kings. The chief priest had performed the Opening of the Mouth ceremony, Neferhotep assisting.

"Thutmose looked every inch a King, riding at the head of the procession," said Dje-Nefer. "Though he did not seem upset that she had died."

"He had been waiting a long time to be Pharaoh," said Bibi.

"I think he will be a very popular Pharaoh."

"Yes, even if some are already suggesting that he killed Hatshepsut." Bibi shook his head. "He had nothing to do with it. Her doctors tried, but nothing worked on that incurable disease."

"I heard His Majesty has said he plans to 'return to our traditional ways.' Mother says that means he has been thinking of how to erase Hatshepsut from our memories."

"Perhaps. I went to her temple a few days ago," said Bibi. "It is still intact, but no one guards it. I watered the myrrh trees. They were dying." He sighed. "Our world is changing."

"Uncle Neferhotep said to tell you that he will be visiting Nubia soon," said Dje-Nefer. "He wants me to come with him when he goes, to study the art in the tombs. It is a little different from what I am used to seeing.."

"Neferhotep would be wise to stay in Nubia," said Bibi.

"Because of Thutmose?" Dje-Nefer asked.

"Many of Her Majesty's friends and advisors have already scattered to other cities."

"Neferhotep is dedicated to Amon-Ra. I doubt he will leave. Mutemwija is thinking of moving there, though."

The sun was lowering, turning blood-red in the dusty air. A gentle cool breeze was rising from the Nile, now restored to its former glory. The white sails of several reed boats glided past in both directions, water droplets glittering off the poles of the sailors.

"I should get back," said Dje-Nefer.

Bibi reached under his traveling cloak. "The Pharaoh asked me to give you something."

"Thutmose?"

"Already you forget?" asked Bibi, chuckling.

"Never!" said Dje-Nefer. "But she already gave us so much."

"This was just for you."

Bibi held out his hand. On his palm lay a stone statuette of Hatshepsut, dressed as a man.

"To remember her by," he said.

"I will," said Dje-Nefer, taking the statuette.

"Keep it safe," said Bibi. "The Pharaoh also had a gift for Mutemwija. In her last hour, she had me take it off her own arm. She said it was something she felt she needed to do."

He reached under his cloak again, then brought out a slim gold bracelet.

"She's here tonight," said Dje-Nefer. "I'll give it to her."

With a nod and a wave, Bibi set off, heading upriver towards Aswan.

Dje-Nefer stroked the statuette.

"Remember." She would. Even if no one else did.

Thanks to a friend she had never met, Dje-Nefer knew that the memory of a great woman would not be erased forever. The name of the female Pharaoh—Hatshepsut—would endure.

Dje-Nefer turned and walked up the long dusty road back to the villa, where her future waited.

Hatshepsut, the female Pharaoh, really did exist. She reigned as King in the Eighteenth Dynasty, from 1490 to 1468 B.C. After her death, her mortuary temple was destroyed, her images smashed, and her obelisks were plastered over. Only a few small fragments remained, enough to give Egyptologists clues to her existence, which they found in the early 1900's. The process of restoring the temple is still underway. The temple itself is one of the loveliest in all of Egypt; with its series of colonnades and ramps, it seems to grow gracefully from the cliff towering at its back. You can still see images of Hatshepsut's trading expeditions to Punt painted on the walls.

No one knows who damaged the temple of the female Pharaoh and tried to remove her name from history, although evidence points to her nephew Thutmose III. Perhaps it was done to make it look as though the kingdom had passed unbroken from father to son.

Hatshepsut's mummy was lost for centuries and feared to have been destroyed along with her temple.

However, it was rediscovered in 2007, and positively identified as Pharaoh Hatshepsut by DNA testing and by the match of a missing tooth, found in a Canopic box marked with her cartouche.

PRONUNCIATION GUIDE

Most of the names for the fictional characters in this book are based on real names of people from Ancient Egypt.

Amon-Ra- Ah mon rah (ah as in "jaw")

Bast- Bahst

Bes- Base

Bibi- Bee bee

Daoud- Dah ood

Dje-Nefer- Jeh nef fer

Drus- Droos

Hapi- Hah pea

Hathor- Hah thor

Hatshepsut- Hat shep soot

Hekhanakhte- Heh kan ak tay

Hopi- Hoe pea

Horus- Hoar uss

Isis- Eye siss

Ka-Aper- Kah Ah per

Kai- Kye

Khufu– Koo foo

Mentmose- Ment mose

Meryt-Re- Meh rit ray

Miw- Mew

Mutemwija- Moo tem wee jah

Neferhotep- Neh fur hoe tep

Osiris- Oh sigh riss

Parahotep- Pair ah hoe tep

Ra- Rah

Ramose- Rah mose

Satyah- Sat yah

Sekhmet- Sek met

Senmut- Sen moot

Tetisheri- Teh tee share ree

Thutmose- Thoot mose

Ti- Tee

This pronunciation guide is only a suggestion. No one knows the exact spelling of names, which are taken from hieroglyphs. The hieroglyphs are vague about vowels, and opinions differ about stressed syllables.

ACKNOWLEDGMENTS

Many thanks to members of the KooKoos critique group: Gloria Singendonk, Trina Wiebe, Alma Fullerton, Lori Robidoux, Lisa Marta and Laurie Brown, who saw the potential of this book in its (very) raw first drafts. Thanks also to my father, whose collection of books inspired my love of all things Egyptian when I was very young. Thanks to Kim Davies, whose timely invitation to join her and several other women on an adventure tour of Egypt allowed me to experience the Black Land for myself. A huge thank you to Linda Duddridge, an invaluable reader and mistake-catcher. Special thanks to editor Madeline Smoot, for her usual terrific advice.

☖ ABOUT THE AUTHOR ☖

Leslie Carmichael has been inside the Great Pyramid at Giza, has watched the world turn purple during a total solar eclipse, and has been an honoured guest at a Canadian-Scottish-Taiwanese wedding. She has swum in the Red Sea, picked amethysts out of the ground near Thunder Bay, watched a space shuttle land, and cooked a Medieval dinner for 200 people. She has worn a corset, a suit of armour and a Klingon outfit (but not all at the same time).

Leslie also writes comic interactive plays for Pegasus Performances. She likes to work on miniature dolls and dollhouses when she's not writing. She can crochet three-dimensional objects without a pattern, but finds knitting way too complicated.

Leslie lives in Calgary, Alberta, with her husband, three children and two cats.